ROY

DEEPTHI L

SUNIL IBRAHIM

BOOKSTHAKAM
TRANSCENDING BOUNDARIES

Published by Booksthakam, India

info@booksthakam.com
www.booksthakam.com

ROY

A Booksthakam Book/ published by arrangement with the author

ISBN-13: 978-93-91850-61-6
Printed and bound in India by Thomson Press India Ltd.

*To all who kept a place in thier heart
for the malayalam movie ROY*

CONTENTS

PROLOGUE
August 19, 2022

Clasping the shoulder straps of her backpack, she looked at the thickly wooded land that lay ahead of her. The tarred road had given way to a jungle. After two tedious bus journeys, any human would have doubtlessly been dead tired. One would have sat there leaning against a tree and perhaps even taken a nap before walking any further. However, her brain was not willing to acknowledge tiredness that evening. In fact, it had shut down every other sensation except that of investigation. She did not even enjoy the beautiful forest trail through which her bus took her. The large trees that arched towards the road were a delight to every pair of eyes inside the vehicle except those of hers. The sight of the monkey with its infant clinging to its chest, which would normally have made her jump from her seat in excitement, completely failed to strike a chord. She only had one thing in mind.

It was dark inside the woods even though the time was only half past five. The uniform and gradual rise in the tone of crickets indicated that they did not like the presence of an intruder in their territory. They seemed to be warning the other members of their species of a potential danger. Even an insect had someone to watch its back while nobody would know if something happened to her there. Not one person had a hint about where to look for her if she went missing.

She slowed down her pace and placed each step carefully as she moved forward through the thick vegetation. The sound of dry, fallen leaves crackling under her shoes echoed all over the wilderness. She turned on the flashlight of her mobile phone and focused the light on the ground to keep herself safe from poisonous beings that might have camouflaged themselves beneath the dead leaves.

The only thing that guided her now was her

intuition. If her people knew why she had set out on her solo trip to this forsaken land, they would never have let her go alone. They would have told her to get a hold of herself and to stop living in her fantasy world. Some of them would also have volunteered to go with her. These were precisely the reasons why she decided to keep the destination and intention of her journey a secret. As always, it was her sole decision not to involve anybody else in this.

She kept on turning back since she had a persistent feeling of being watched. Dusk was also setting in, giving the place a much more sinister look. Soon, the whole area would be engulfed in pitch black. She realized that she would have to end her search shortly and find a place to stay for the night. Before calling it a day, she decided to go a little further in the hope of finding at least something that she could call a clue. Using both her hands, she softly moved aside the branches and creepers that blocked her way. She might have proceeded some fifty meters when she spotted a tiled roof of what looked like an abandoned structure hidden among the thickets. Her eyes widened. She took out her mobile phone from the back pocket of her jeans without taking her eyes off the building.

Suddenly, she felt as if someone pushed her from behind. Losing her balance, she fell flat on her stomach and hit her head on something hard. The last thing she remembered was a sharp pain on her forehead and a ringing sound inside her ears that was slowly fading.

PART 1

Teena

May 2012

CHAPTER 1

The aesthetically designed stone wall building of Divine Hospital, with the backdrop of the breathtaking view of Munnar hills, looked more like a resort than a hospital. Coming here in the evening after my classes to pick up Ashwathy had become a daily routine. I parked my two-wheeler on the hospital premises, walked inside and peered into the doctor's room. Ashwathy was standing in her doctor's coat with her notepad in one hand, reading out a patient's medical history to her senior doctor. When she saw me standing half-hidden behind the door, she gestured for me to wait for some time.

I sat outside on a bench in the corridor, thinking of taking out the book that I had borrowed from the college library. Just as I was about to open my bag, I spotted a man sitting opposite me, reading a book. While a person with a book was itself an uncommon sight, a person with a book in a hospital waiting area was indeed a rare spectacle. He appeared to be in his late twenties or early thirties. His blue checkered shirt which was tucked in matched his white jeans. The neatly combed hair and the perfectly trimmed beard along with his grave demeanour gave him an air of mystery.

I tilted my head in an attempt to see the cover of the book. The man's eyes moved gracefully from its pages to meet my eyes. Keeping his finger inside the book to mark the page that he was reading, he shut it and lifted it in such a way that I could clearly see its title – *The History of Love* by Nicole Krauss. I was taken aback and rather embarrassed that he saw me looking at him. However, in an attempt to hide my unease, I smiled at him and signalled that the book was good. He did not smile back at me. With his face impassive, he looked at me for another second before returning to his book.

I had a strong desire to talk to him. In an attempt to regain his attention, I took out my book from my bag. Opening it slowly, I checked whether he was watching me. His eyes once again moved gently from his book to mine. I succeeded. I was about to grab the opportunity and start a conversation when Ashwathy came out of the room. "Let's go," she said as she hurried outside. I followed her reluctantly. As I was about to pass the waiting space, I turned to look at him once more. He already had his nose in the book.

We rode through the familiar curvy road adorned with tea plantations on both sides. It had been one year since Ashwathy and I rented a paying guest accommodation together in Munnar. From the time I first met her at MCN Public School, Kottayam, at the age of ten, she had been destined to listen to my eccentric theories and fanciful notions. This time also it was no different.

"I felt something special about that man," I said loudly leaning back slightly towards her.

"Which man?" she asked, clueless.

"That man, the one who was sitting opposite me in the hospital. Didn't you see him?"

"Oh! Him," she said casually. "He comes often. I have seen him before."

We reached our room and Ashwathy opened the door while I parked my scooter in the shed. She went inside immediately to take a hot shower as was her custom after she came back from what she called, 'her struggle with germs'. I made coffee for both of us and added two spoons of sugar to her cup. The refreshing, bitter-sweet aroma of coffee filled the air.

"Either I have seen him before or I will see him again," I said as Ashwathy and I sat in front of our respective cups of piping hot coffee.

"Whom?" she asked, taking a bite from her digestive biscuit.

I looked at her disbelievingly. "The one I was talking about, the hospital guy!"

"You're still thinking about him?" she asked.

"He didn't seem like someone who reads English romantic novels," I said, dreamily.

"He didn't seem like someone who reads books at all!" she countered.

"If you had come a little late, I would definitely have gone and talked to him."

"You're crazy!" She shook her head to show her disapproval.

"Haven't you heard of *déjà vu*?" I continued, ignoring her rebuke.

"The feeling that you had experienced certain things earlier, but you are actually experiencing them for the first time," she answered as if I was her professor asking her to define the term.

"I have a theory about that," I said.

"I am so sorry, Teena. I have a lot of work to do," she said, getting up with her coffee mug and walking hastily into the bedroom.

CHAPTER 2

I had my own theories about everything. I chose to think of the rainbow more as a magic of nature than as the scattering of light. I have been deemed crazy by many who listened to them but I treasured my theories. After all, what fun was there in life if not for some irrational and groundless ideas? Perhaps, they were what fuelled the writer in me.

The library was the most deserted place on the whole campus of the Institute of Journalism. Except for me and the librarian Anitha, there was not a single human being in this part of the college. As usual, I was in my personal corner near the window, but contrary to my habit, I had no book in front of me. I felt refreshed as I sat looking at the tall tree, the name of which was unknown to me, through the windows covered in fog.

My theory which was heartlessly dismissed by my friend was still stuck in my mind. The words were struggling within me, dying to get expressed. I chuckled as I remembered the lines of Margaret Atwood that I read recently,

'& in labour, her thighs tied

together by the enemy.'

I opened a blank page of my notepad and started with the date.

29.05.2012

Déjà vu

A newborn sleeps most of the time, doesn't it? I believe it is because it cannot take in everything that it sees around after coming from the peaceful darkness of its mother's womb. However, if we observe it when it sleeps, we can see that it smiles and moves its limbs. What would it be dreaming about? My theory is that during our infant stage, we experience things in our sleep that we will actually experience some time in the near or distant future. A baby sees people in its dream in the same form that it is meant to meet them in real life. That is why we see babies showing affection towards certain people even when they have only just met them. The adult world has given this a name, *déjà vu*. According to me, we get to feel *déjà vu* because, when we were babies, in our dreams, we have been in that situation or we have seen that person. Yesterday, I got the taste of *déjà vu* for the first time in my life.

I was relieved after pouring it all out. I closed my notepad and pen and walked out of the library. Stepping into the cold passage that led to the grounds, I took out my mobile phone. I wanted an immediate help from Ashwathy.

"Hello," she said in a hushed tone, picking up at the very first ring.

"Hey, this is urgent. I need your help," I said.

"What is it?" she asked.

"Can you get me the details of that man from your hospital records?"

"Don't you have anything better to do?" she snapped. "Why don't you attend your classes and study for a change?"

"I am doing journalism and not medicine," I replied without losing my cool. "Will you get me the details or not?"

"Fine!" she retorted.

I attended the final hour which was the session on reporting. I never skipped reporting classes since it was given by Professor Parvathy. She had a unique way of capturing and retaining the attention of even a person with a wandering mind like me. That was the only hour of the day when my brain completely focused on something.

"That's it for today. Hope you guys have a wonderful evening."

I put my books inside my bag and rushed out after saying a quick goodbye to my classmates. Unlike other days, I was the first to reach the parking lot since my curiosity was eating me up. The soothing warmth of the evening sun kissed my face but I did not have time to enjoy it. I squeezed my scooter through the other vehicles and somehow managed to get myself out of the campus.

The Divine Hospital seemed more crowded than ever that evening. I walked towards the hospital canteen which stood next to the main building. The canteen was almost empty except for two people who had already stood up to leave. I sent an SMS to Ashwathy, *'At the canteen'*, and ordered a strong coffee without sugar. Ashwathy reached within some minutes and sat opposite me. Without further ado, she began, keeping her voice down.

"I didn't see his file in the general medicine department but I enquired some more and got his files from two other departments." I leaned forward, listening intently. "His name is Roy Jacob. He comes regularly to see the psychiatrist. It is mentioned that he has some serious dream problem which has not been properly diagnosed." She took a sip from my coffee and protruded her tongue to show her disgust at the bitterness. She looked at me with creased brows as if asking me how I drank my coffee like that and continued. "I couldn't get anything more from the psychiatry department. They have kept most of their information confidential." "What about the other one?" I inquired. "It is an old file about an IVF treatment. He has no sperm count. He cannot have kids. I heard that he got divorced soon after that," she paused and added, "You better steer clear of him."

CHAPTER 3

Roy Jacob was not a unique name. Finding some information about my *déjà vu* man would never have been easy if I had lived before the era of social media. I typed the letters in the search bar of Facebook and realised that many of the numerous Roy Jacobs who existed around the world had Facebook accounts. To make my task easier, I applied a filter and chose the city as Munnar. The page blinked and refreshed itself. There was only one result. A Facebook profile without a face.

I moved my cursor towards the faceless face and clicked on it. A page with next to nothing greeted me from my laptop screen. I suddenly saw something on the side of the page, a piece of information which was more than vital to me.

Librarian at the Institute of Journalism,

Munnar

I sat inside the same college library, grinning at the screen. A chill ran down my spine when I thought about the likelihood that this Roy Jacob could be my *déjà vu* man. My hands and legs were shivering in anticipation. I stood up and walked to the reception desk with a thumping heart. I knew just the person to approach for my answers.

Librarian Anitha and I had always been on friendly terms since I was the only regular visitor to the library. She was appointed a year before I joined the college. I developed a good rapport with her from my very first day. She had once told me something about the former librarian. Something about why he was terminated from his job.

"Anitha, can you spare a few minutes?" I requested.

"Sure," she said, looking up from the newspaper on her table.

"Can I find a picture of the previous librarian somewhere?"

"Hmm…" She bit her lips and lowered her eyes to the floor as she took a moment to think.

"I think there is a picture in last year's college magazine. It would be there in the topmost row," she said pointing towards the magazine rack.

Without wasting another second, I proceeded towards the rack and ran my eyes over the various magazine covers on the top row. I read the names that were both familiar and unfamiliar to me and found the one I was looking for. A panoramic picture of the college's main building with its well-cropped grass and the stunning background of the mountains shrouded in mist made the cover page an eye-catcher even as it sat amidst the latest editions of some popular magazines. Institute of Journalism was written in a small font above the mountain and the name *Reflections* was written below it in a larger font. Showing a thumbs-up to Anitha, I sat on a nearby chair and opened the page where they had printed the photographs. I turned each page impatiently, skim-reading the descriptions below the photographs, and stopped at the one which said 'Non-teaching staff'. I kept my finger on each face, ticking each one off to make sure that I did not miss him. After quite a tiring labour of my eyes, I located him in the middle of the second row with the sombre expression that I had perceived when I saw him at the hospital.

All at once, the whole place looked very different. I realised that I was occupying the room where he once used to work five days every week from morning to evening. I was now spending most of my time in the very same space where he used to spend most of his time. This room knew him. He had given this place his most valuable asset, his time. These walls had witnessed his happiness, his sorrow, his anger, his frustration, and his embarrassment in the same way as they had seen mine. He had once breathed this air that I was breathing now. He had left a part of himself here, in this library. I had seen him before, though not with my eyes. I had breathed him and sensed him with my skin. My being, which hovered in this room now, was eternally intertwined with that of his.

"What kind of a person was he?" I asked, turning to Anitha.

"Well, I don't know much about him. I have just heard that he was sacked because he was not in his right mind."

"Do you know if he had any friends here?"

"I am not sure. I think he used to go to the canteen. The canteen owner once asked me why he lost his job. Maybe someone there knows," she said.

I stared at her while my mind processed the things she said.

"Why did you ask about him? Is there any problem?" she asked.

"No," I said. "No, nothing. I saw him once and he seemed peculiar. Just curious, that's it."

She was still looking at me doubtfully when I waved to her and walked out of the library. Each day of my investigation brought me closer to Roy. There was absolutely no logic in what I was doing. Nobody would have gone after someone whom they had seen only once. But my conviction that he was going to be somebody in my life was growing stronger. I was determined to know more about him.

CHAPTER 4

I sipped my bitter coffee and pretended to be reading something from my mobile phone. The canteen was crowded. Every college canteen would have at least one table occupied by a noisy group at its peak time. They would laugh boisterously, bang at the table with their hands and make fun of each other. They would be unaware of the frowning faces that periodically turned towards them or the curse words that emanated in low voices from between parted lips. For them, the table was their own momentary world where nobody else existed.

I ordered two small banana fritters so as not to invite the scornful stare from the canteen employees. I had to keep on having something if I wanted to wait there till the crowd was manageable. To kill the time, I looked at the greying walls with white patches and tried to imagine shapes in them. One of them looked like a man falling head first from a height. Below him was another one, which resembled a river. I watched the man who would eternally be falling into the river without ever touching its water, like Keats' lover engraved in the Grecian urn who could never kiss his beloved. A waiter in a pale yellow shirt and a green lungi folded above his knees brought me my order and went to the next table before I could even say 'thank you'. I bit the corner of one of my banana fritters and realised that it was not a bad idea to order some food after all. The sweet taste of fried, ripe banana reminded me of the needs of my stomach.

People who were there when I entered began to leave one by one and after half an hour, the noisy gang cleared out as well. I put the last piece of the banana fritter into my mouth and wiped my oily fingers on the piece of newspaper which they provided with the snack. I quickly approached the cash desk with the handwritten bill given to me by the waiter. The owner of the place, a middle-aged man dressed similar to the waiter, sat behind an old wooden table on which there were bottles of peanut candies, sesame balls, toffees and other sweets. He was collecting money and exchanging pleasantries with a customer who had come to buy a parcel. I waited till she left and moved closer to the table with my bill.

"How was the food?" he asked, beaming.

"It was nice," I replied.

"Please do visit often," he said as he kept the money I gave him inside the drawer.

"Umm... I came to know that you are acquainted with the earlier librarian, Roy Jacob," I said coming to the point straight away.

"Yes," he said. "He lost his job last year, right?"

"Yeah. Do you have his contact number?"

"He gave it to me once. Wait, let me see." He squinted his eyes slightly as he started checking his mobile phone.

"How was he to you, I mean, were you close to him?" I asked while he continued going through the contacts on his phone.

"Not that much but he used to visit frequently. For lunch and tea. He was a peculiar man, knew a lot of things."

"Have you talked to him?"

"We used to talk, yes. He used to speak about a variety of topics. Things I haven't even thought about. Ah, here it is! Can you please write it down yourself? I have a problem with my eyesight."

"Sure," I said and typed the number on my mobile phone, saving it as Roy Jacob.

"I have often marvelled at how he came to know such a lot of things," he continued. "A brilliant man. But three years back, he gradually started withdrawing into himself. I heard that he got divorced last year or something."

The question that I dreaded, why I wanted to know about Roy, did not come from him. I was not actually afraid of the question. Thrilled as I was on the prospect of calling my mystery man soon, I did not feel like standing there and explaining to the canteen owner what made me interested in Roy. I smiled and nodded at him and he politely returned the gesture.

I had Roy's number with me. All I had to do was press the call button. I badly wanted to know if Roy felt the same way as I did that day. It was so unlike me to think twice about something I wanted to do but I was concerned if I would be trespassing into his privacy. I ambled down the cemented road that led to the lover's path, kicking the dried leaves on my way. Passing the beautiful street lamps that were designed like those in the Victorian era, I sat on an empty bench and looked at Roy's number. I could not help but call and take a chance. I boldly pressed the call button. It rang for some time before he picked up.

"Hello." I heard his melancholic voice for the first time.

"Hello," I responded.

CHAPTER 5

I had lifted the helmet visor to let the pure, cool hill station breeze touch my face. The lush green plantations with silver oak trees standing tall and proud among them seemed new to me that day. The afternoon sun shone on the leaves giving them an unusual glow. It looked as if the flora had put on a new garb to celebrate the occasion of our first real meeting.

Talking to Roy over the phone was easier than I expected. He did not appear in the least surprised by my call. He talked to me as if he was only continuing a conversation that we had left midway. I grabbed the opportunity and asked him if we could meet for a coffee when I learned that he had the habit of taking a stroll in the park near my college every day. When he accepted my invitation without even a word of protest, I was on cloud nine.

I saw him passing the gates of the park at the same time that I reached and I stopped my scooter by his side. "Hi," I said, greeting him with a smile. He looked at me and gave a small nod which my eyes would have missed had they not been carefully watching him. His lips refused to curve into a smile as if they had forgotten how to

I parked the vehicle inside and waited for him. When he reached, he motioned me that we would walk towards the café. "You're early," he said, checking his watch. I smiled again. "This hour's session is given by Professor Parvathy, isn't it? Didn't you want to attend?" I looked at him, not bothering to conceal my astonishment. "After a whole year you still remember the timetable?" I asked. "You told me you loved her classes," he said, his expression not changing a bit. I stopped dead in my tracks. "Yeah, her classes are awesome and I usually make sure that I don't miss them. But when did I tell you all these?"

Roy opened the door for me. 'Chivalrous!' I thought to myself. We moved towards a small oval-shaped table near the window which had two chairs placed on either end. It was the only spot which gave the perfect view of the garden outside.

The waiter came immediately and stood beside us to take our order.

"One tea and a strong coffee without sugar," he said before I could even open my mouth.

"Did you order that coffee for me?" I asked.

He nodded.

"Roy, tell me the truth. Do you have some mind-reading skills or something?"

This time, it was he who looked at me in what could be read as amazement in his generally expressionless eyes.

"You ordered it a few days back at the hospital canteen. I thought you might be diabetic," he said.

"No, I am not!" I said, laughing. "I like its bitter taste. I don't want to tone it down with sugar."

"There is something sweet in that bitterness," he said.

"Exactly!" I paused and said, "But how did

you see that I ordered coffee? I didn't see you anywhere near me!"

"You asked me to join you for a coffee at the canteen. We were together," he said without an ounce of mischief on his face.

"I am sorry, but this is the first time that we are meeting after we saw each other at the hospital waiting area. Remember? The day you showed me your book."

"Is that so?" he asked dubiously. "Then it must have been a dream."

The waiter came with our order. Roy took a small sip from his scalding tea after blowing into it. He looked out of the window staring at a group of small birds walking on the grass. I understood that this might be the problem that Ashwathy said he had. I thought of something to say that could cheer him up.

"What else did you see in your dream?" I asked. He turned towards me looking amazed. Nobody might have shown any interest in his dreams before.

"You didn't allow me to say anything. You

kept on talking," he said.

"Okay, what all did I tell you?" I asked.

"You told me that you never missed Professor Parvathy's lectures."

"Mm-hmm."

"You told me about your best friend Ashwathy who works at the hospital, you told me about your love for books."

"That's cool! Your dreams, they are like… like magic!"

He sipped his tea without another word and went back to watching the birds. I too looked out of the window savouring the scenery. There was nothing awkward about the silence between Roy and me. We did not try to fill in the moment with words. I felt that we were forming a deep connection in that quietude which was beyond anything that any conversation could hope to create. I did not know much about this person sitting on the other side of my table; neither did I know anything about the mental ailment that he was suffering from. But I knew that there was something between him and me that could not be confined within the existing labels. Rather, a relationship that was yet to be given a name.

CHAPTER 6

"I believe you stopped going after the hospital guy. You haven't talked about him ever since the day I told you about his issues."

Ashwathy asked as she was removing her books and her laptop from her bed and was preparing to retire for the day. I instantly closed the book that I was trying to concentrate on and sat up on my bed. I was yearning to talk about Roy to her but was holding myself back since she had warned me against him. I kept the book on the bedside table and prepared myself to narrate the story without getting bashed by her.

"Do you know where I spend most of my time at college?" I asked.

"The library, for sure. You have never been

fond of lectures," she said.

"Right! And you know what, Roy used to work in the same library!" I exclaimed, excitedly scanning her face for a similar reaction.

"So you have seen him before?" she asked, confused.

"No! He was dismissed before I joined," I said, feeling slightly dejected that she did not get my point even though deep inside I knew that she would not.

"I now spend most of my time in the space where he once used to sit all day for many years!" I explained.

Ashwathy looked at me with contempt written all over her face as she understood that this was another one of my 'nonsensical' narratives.

"I enquired about him in college and heard some things that interested me. I took his number, arranged a meeting..."

"What!" Ashwathy cut in.

"And we met. It was wonderful," I said without

even stopping to breathe.

She glared at me in disbelief, not taking her eyes off me for a whole minute. 'What did I tell you?' her eyes asked me. She removed her slippers and sat on her bed facing me. "So, what are the further plans?" she asked. "We didn't talk much during our first meeting. So, I have asked him to come to the college tomorrow afternoon," I said, avoiding her eyes. "I should have known," she said after a moment of silence, her contempt turning into hopelessness. "Goodnight," she said as she lay down on her bed and turned to the other side, facing the wall.

Mornings were the most beautiful hours of the day if you lived in a hill station. I would never be tired of the damp mornings in Munnar. It would almost be eleven when you began to feel the temperature of the sun here, unlike the other places in Kerala which would start heating up much earlier. Back home in Ernakulam, a district situated in the middle part of Kerala, I had to wear my driving gloves to protect myself from the scorching heat of the sun while here I looked forward to feeling the sun on my hands. Even though the distance between them was less than

130 km, the two places were like two different worlds.

I had many things to ask Roy. I wanted to know more about him. Somebody always bewitched time to take a slow pace every time I was thrilled about something. I sat through the first hour in college but I could not concentrate. After an hour, when the lecturer walked out and I was brought back into reality from the enchantment of a daydream, I realised I was having mental conversations with Roy. The enigma that he was made me more and more curious.

After lunch, I went and sat in the library just as I had told him the other day. I checked my watch every fifteen minutes, willing the time to pass quickly. After what seemed like ages, a message notification came on my mobile phone.

Reached

I spotted Roy at the entrance of the library as soon as I got the message. I stood up and waved at him. He raised his hand in acknowledgement. A teacher who stood searching for something in the reference section gazed alternately at him and me.

A myriad of questions might have popped up in her mind. Roy nodded at Anitha when he saw her behind her computer gaping at us. She returned an awkward smile and turned her head towards me. I blinked at her.

The ex-librarian was nervous. He looked around his old kingdom, possibly trying to rekindle his bond with his inanimate friends. I urged him to walk between shelves and showed him my favourite section. As the smell of old books began to touch his nostrils, he started unwinding bit by bit. He ran the back of his hand through the books as though he was caressing the cheeks of his beloved. There, I observed for the first time, the passionate side of the otherwise unemotional man.

"Shall we go out?" he asked.

CHAPTER 7

Kundala Lake was the only site in Munnar that I had never explored. Roy was surprised that I had not seen that heaven. I sat beside him in his old green Premier Padmini car as we drove through a bridge leading to our destination. Vintage cars always held a special place in my heart. The contemporary four-wheelers did not possess the majesty that they had. Like everything modern, the present-day cars with their incredible features could not even hope to compete with the beauty of the classic ones. Roy parked the car by the side of the road and we started to walk.

I could not believe what welcomed me. The towering eucalyptus trees that skirted the sides of the road starting from the end of the bridge were only the tip of the iceberg when it came to the elegance of the place. Everything around was green. The peaceful lake that flowed horizontally began to be visible as we took our steps forward. The water reflected the colour of the foliage on both its sides. Small green hills that appeared to be pleased with themselves stood out among the plants.

Roy and I sat on the trunk of a fallen eucalyptus tree. Apart from us, there was only a family of four; a father, mother, son and daughter, who were waiting on the bank of the lake in their lifejackets for the boatman to prepare their boat. The girl was jumping up and down unable to contain her enthusiasm while the boy stood hugging his father's leg. The mother had her hand on her son's head.

The afternoon sun that held the region inside its tender embrace cast a warm spell in the same way that a bonfire did during a cold night. Land and water looked inseparable like a pair of twins lying hand in hand inside a cradle. The air stroked everything living and non-living as it moved smoothly and powerfully at the same time. Minutes passed as we sat in silence.

"Shall I ask you something?" I asked Roy as he sat watching the family ride the boat.

"Yes," he said, turning his head to look at me.

"Water, air, fire, land, which one would you choose?" I asked

"Why?"

"Let me see how romantic you are," I said.

"Water," he replied.

"Water! Yes!" I said clapping my hands in victory.

He tilted his head showing his interest in listening to me more.

"I guessed right!" I continued. "It describes you well. See the lake, it is very composed when it is viewed from here but one gets to know its depth only when one steps into it. The depth can even suck you in."

Roy's body language spoke that he was absorbed in what I was saying which encouraged me to speak more.

"And water can take many shapes and forms. It is adaptive. In the glaciers it is solid; in the rivers, lakes, oceans and seas, it is liquid. The water from such bodies evaporates and becomes water vapour which condenses to form clouds and the same water showers as rain when the clouds become saturated."

He nodded, thinking about it.

"This calm water that we see in front of us can even turn into floods and tsunamis," I concluded, looking into his dark brown eyes.

He looked back at me and smiled slightly.

Roy smiled! I never thought he could smile. I had believed it to be a skill that he lacked. He looked much more handsome now. Even though the smile died after some seconds it was born, I felt like he gifted me something that he had not given to anybody else for a long time.

"And what about land, air and fire?" he asked.

"Land is passive; listens to everyone, keeps secrets. It is patient and tolerant. Haven't you noticed land being compared to women? The concept of Bhumidevi, Mother Earth, is based on it. The goddess of the land is supposed to be the symbol of endurance. Well, I don't personally feel it right, but you got it, didn't you?"

"Yes."

"Yeah," I said. "Land helps everything grow, nourishing whatever comes into contact with it. Land is also a mystery. Land doesn't easily show its emotions unless provoked. But don't take it for granted, unless you want a landslide."

He almost grinned this time, surprising me even more. He was like a book that captivated a reader as its plot unfolded little by little. A book that you kept close by all the time and re-read even after finishing it since you knew there was always going to be something somewhere that you missed.

"Now, air," I continued. "Air is transient. You can't expect it to stay. It is not permanent. Still, it can be a fierce hurricane at times."

"Mm-hmm," he said, without taking his eyes off me.

"And, fire. Passionate. Very passionate, but dies down soon. It burns everything that associates with it."

"Nice thoughts," he said. "You can be a good author. Try your hand at fiction. You know, apart from journalistic writing."

"I want to become an author. Maybe not immediately but I will definitely publish my novels one day. I have some ideas in here." I touched the side of my forehead with my index finger.

He smiled again and I had a hunch that I would see it quite often.

I never asked anyone about their personal lives as it was the part of an individual that I was least interested in. However, when I sat there that day with Roy, I could feel my heart yearning to know everything about him. On the other hand, I also did not want to spoil the beautiful moment by bringing in topics which would make things unpleasant or even discomfiting. *Let everything take its own pace*, I told myself.

I expected Roy to speak more but he did not. He suddenly looked as if he was dismayed. Realising that he preferred to go back into his shell, I decided not to bombard him with any more questions. We resumed watching the family as they returned and alighted one by one. The parents cautiously helped the children to get down. They ran as soon as their feet touched the ground while the elders struggled to keep up with their energy. The tranquillity was broken by the kids' laughter and howls. The sound of their rapid footsteps echoed all over and was amplified because of the stillness of the woods.

The time which was enchanted worked reversely when I wanted it to stay still. I glanced at my watch, hoping against hope that it was not anywhere near five yet. But the bewitcher had his way. It was time to go back.

"Roy, we must get going. I have to take my scooter before six," I said reluctantly.

We walked back up the sloped way. The murmuring of the Kundala Lake was receding from my ears. We walked past the eucalyptus trees and I spotted the colour of Roy's car which could be mistaken for another group of plants amidst the greenery. He started the car as soon as we got inside. I noticed that he was still not ready for another conversation and decided to give him the space that he needed. As I rolled down the window and looked at the road, I began contemplating the meaning of his silence and of the several unspoken words that I saw in his eyes, hoping that I would be able to delve deep into him soon.

CHAPTER 8

Roy was waiting for me on his doorstep as I slowed down my scooter, searching for his house. His home looked old and charming like his car. The stone walls reminded me of the Divine Hospital where we first met. The white door and windows and the light peach-coloured curtains that were visible through the door and window glasses complemented the natural colour of the stones. An antique, wired chair was placed in the sit-out by the side of the main entrance. Going inside those rusty gates was like entering a time machine through which I travelled back a century.

It had been two days since we visited Kundala Lake. I thought that it would be good to give him some space even though it was difficult for me not to contact him. Today morning I called and asked him the directions to his house. I did not feel in the least odd about what I was doing.

Roy came down the steps beaming at me. He was not stingy with that facial gesture anymore, nor was I stunned each time I saw it. It was as though I had always been accustomed to his ways; his blank face and the sudden sprouting of emotions in it, his smile that lasted only for a very short time and his eyes that were always uncertain about everything they saw. We had only met five days back but nothing about him was unfamiliar to me now.

As soon as I set foot inside the house, I saw that the interior was not as artistic as the exterior. There was an old wooden wired sofa set without cushions in the living room. In front of it was a plain, wooden teapoy. A table sat in the corner between the two sofas on which there were more than a score of books, shabbily stacked one over the other. I could find no plants or decorative pieces anywhere. However, there was not even a speck of dust in the room. He had taken care to keep his abode clean.

Roy went into the kitchen to get me

something to drink while I examined his books, checking each cover and description. I was astonished to see that the table contained a piece of many nations around the globe. All the books kept on it were gems in world literature. There were English translations of even Greek and Italian works. While I used to boast that I was an avid reader, I realised on that day that I was nothing but a novice.

"You like my books?" he asked as he came with coffee in two glass tumblers.

"What a collection! There are some names that I haven't even heard of," I said. "I am ashamed to call myself a reader."

"Don't be," he said. "I didn't know about them when I was your age."

Roy kept the glasses on the teapoy and stood near me as I carried on admiring the books. I carefully took out the copy of *Things Fall Apart* from the pile and held it in my hand.

"Can I borrow this? I always wanted to read it."

"Sure," he said. "There are more books inside.

You can check them out whenever you want."

I thanked him and sat down on the sofa with the book. He sat on the other sofa next to me. I took a small sip from my coffee and was pleased that he remembered my preference.

"Have you always lived in Munnar?" I asked.

"No," he said. "I am from Alappuzha."

"Do you ever go there now?" I asked.

"No."

"Why?"

"I have no friends there," he replied.

"Do you have friends here?" I asked.

He just smiled in response, glancing down at his feet.

We travelled through plenty of subjects as they came one after the other. Not a single meaningless sentence passed between us. Books, movies, college, professors, nature, all featured in our conversation. For both souls, it was a fulfilling and gratifying experience. Roy completely let go of whatever was holding him back. He was not at all conscious. Words came out as easily and involuntarily as thoughts.

The open windows invited the fog inside. I enjoyed its soft chilliness and asked Roy to let the windows remain open. The curtains moved in a specific rhythm in the gentle breeze, creating waves in the air. The room was filled with the scent of books and outdoor plants which was carried inside by the wind.

We were unaware of the approaching night. We might have inadvertently believed that we could put a harness on the Earth if we did not look outside. Despite what we fancied, the Earth went on rotating and the blackness began to creep in until it nearly swallowed everything around. Finally, I checked my watch.

"It's already 7. I need to go before it gets any darker."

Roy followed me as I darted outside. I got on my scooter, turned on the headlight, kicked up the side stand, started it and looked back at the house with its master standing beside the front door. The mournful expression was back on his face. I smiled and instantly reversed everything I did; switched off the light, turned off the ignition, pushed back the side stand and got down from the vehicle.

CHAPTER 9

The bliss that I saw in his eyes was enough for me to know that he did not want me to go either. As always, I did not give it a second thought. I ran to him and planted a deep kiss on his bearded cheek. The smell of his skin intoxicated me with a kind of pleasure that I had not experienced before. I pulled him gently inside and closed the door. He gazed at me as if I was a dream. I closed my eyes, held both his hands and led them to my cheeks to encourage him to kiss me. It took a few seconds before he pulled me to him and I felt his dry lips on my forehead. He was still looking at me in incredulity when I opened my eyes. I smiled reassuringly to convey that everything was fine. He brought my face closer to him again, gave a peck on my nose and went on boldly to my lips. We kissed each other passionately for what seemed like a minute, pausing only to catch our breaths. He then held me inside his soft hug as if he were a little child protecting his dearest toy. I started to feel a comfortable heat in spite of the cold weather.

Suddenly, to my surprise, he lifted me in his arms. He observed me to see if I was okay with what he was doing. I placed my face on his chest to show my consent. I let my face rest there, in the warmth of his chest, listening to the rapid beatings of his heart, as he headed slowly to his bedroom. The dancing curtains patted my hair as he carried me past them. He placed me gently on the bed and got on it himself. The bewilderment in his eyes had not vanished completely. "Is this real?" he asked. I saw that his eyes had started to well up. "It is," I replied. I bid him to come closer to me and looked intently at his face to make him understand how much I longed for him.

He removed the shrug that I was wearing, revealing my noodle-strap top, and ran his fingers smoothly over my shoulders. I could read the love that was brimming within him in the way he looked at me. The serene water was becoming a tsunami. He kissed my forehead again and started exploring me with his lips. He went down the nose, stopped at my lips and travelled to my cleavage. I took off his t-shirt and touched his bare skin. I further leaned towards his shoulders and breathed in his scent. "I love you, Roy," I whispered. He cradled me on his chest and stroked my hair. I remained like that for some time relishing the touch of his fingers, before I fell asleep concentrating on the rhythmic rise and fall.

When I opened my eyes in the morning, Roy was not beside me. I had not seen his room yesterday since we had not bothered to turn on the lights. The bedroom was small. A large cupboard and a writing desk and chair crammed into it made it look much smaller. Opposite them, I saw a brown shirt and a white *mundu* which were hung on a hanger hook on the wall. As I lay lazily looking around, I heard the tap running inside the bathroom. The door opened and Roy came out, wiping his face with a towel.

"Why are you looking at me like that?" I asked when I noted him staring at me.

"Nobody else has ever barged into my life like this. They have only left me," he said. "Even my wife couldn't stay."

"I can't fathom how a woman left someone as romantic as you!" I said.

"It has got nothing to do with romance. She might have had enough." He opened the cupboard, determination visible on his face. "I'll show you something."

I sat up on the bed and tied my hair in a quick bun. Roy took out a file from a drawer inside the cupboard and extended it towards me. I opened it and observed that it contained some papers which were his medical reports from various hospitals. I could see that he was going to confess to me about his health. I scanned through the pages, trying to find out what exactly he wanted me to know.

He pulled up a chair and sat near me. "I have a disorder," he began. I looked up from the file and listened. "I went to many renowned specialists but none was able to diagnose it properly. Whereas I found it out."

He drank some water from a jug kept below the bed and continued.

"I have a messed up brain. I cannot distinguish between reality, dreams and imagination." He subtly searched my face to study my reaction.

"Isn't it fun?" I asked.

He sighed deeply.

"Let me give you an example. If what happened between us last night… if it was a dream or a figment of my imagination and I confused it with reality? Can you guess what will transpire?" He examined my expression again and continued. "I might approach you in the same way the next time I see you and it will end everything between us."

There was a strange stillness in the air. I kept on staring at him, trying to comprehend each of the statements that he made. It was then that I came to know the enormity of his anguish. I was at a loss for words.

"I'll make you a cup of coffee," he said.

I watched him as he went to the kitchen. Nothing he said had changed my feelings for him. I washed my face, put on my shrug, tidied up my hair and headed to the kitchen myself. When I reached, he had already poured the coffee into two glass tumblers and was waiting for me.

"My condition is not as simple as you think," he started to explain more. "It is difficult for a person like me to socialise. It was because of my illness that I was terminated from my job. Even people who were dear to me were scared to be with me. You can't blame my ex-wife for leaving either."

We moved together towards the living room. I sat on the sofa and kept my half-empty glass on the teapoy. Roy went and stood near the window with his back to me. I knew that he was facing away from me as did not want me to see his emotions.

"All I want in my life is not to become a menace to anyone. You asked me why I never go to Alappuzha, didn't you? Well, here's the answer. Just to spare people the trouble," he said, his voice faintly shaking. "Even when I live as discreetly as possible and try to be as careful as I can, sometimes things get out of hand and I become a lunatic in front of the public."

I had already become my usual self even

before he finished his story. Walking up to him in an instant, I hugged him from behind. His body shuddered. I resolutely held him closer to me and tightened my grip around him.

"We live only once. There is no need to be ordinary and boring," I said.

PART 2

Roy

**August 16, 2022 to
August 20, 2022**

CHAPTER 10

The call was picked up immediately and Teena's voice spoke from the other end of the line.

"Hello!"

Ten years of our marriage had completely changed my life. The house that I lived in turned into a home in the real sense of the word. With cushioned sofas and well-arranged tables and chairs, everything looked appealing. Every corner of my, no, our house in Munnar was now occupied by a plant. I spent my time taking care of them and reading the books that Teena and I bought every month when we went to the town together. Those plants and books had always been the sole witnesses to my life which was a constant wait for Fridays for my wife's arrival. They kept me company during the weekdays when Teena was in Ernakulam where she worked as the associate editor for the magazine *VibesToday*.

Teena never failed to take care of me even when she was away. I was not confused by the things happening around me anymore. She distinguished the facts and the fiction for me. To avoid any sort of trouble from my side, in an attempt to be extra careful, I made it a habit not to step out of the gates when she was not here. As I said, everything changed. Everything except one. The happiness that I felt each time I listened to her voice.

"Hey," I said. "Did you catch the train?"

"No, I had to stay back at the office today. Had some immediate work to finish. Don't worry," she added. "Deepak will drop me at the highway. I'll easily get a bus from there."

"Give me a ring half an hour before you arrive, I'll come and pick you up at the bus stop."

"You don't need to. Just keep the key by the window and go to sleep. I'll be there next to you when you wake up."

"Okay."

"Goodnight, Roy."

"Goodnight."

I kept my phone on the side table and retired to bed. Teena's schedules were hectic. She had signed a contract with her friend Deepak's publishing house, Booksthakam Publishers, for her debut novel. Her novel and her work life kept her busy. I felt terrible each time I thought about my inability to go to work and support her dreams, even though she had told me that she was wholly contented with her life. I drifted off to sleep as I lay thinking.

The bathroom door creaked lightly as Teena opened it, rubbing the tip of her hair with a towel. She lay down next to me and rested her head on my chest, a habit which she developed from the first day we slept together. I started wrapping my hands around her when I noticed a small scratch on her elbow.

"Did you fall off the scooter again?" I asked.

"Leave it, Roy, it's nothing," she said, snatching her hand away playfully.

"You have to be more careful, Teena. Riding a

two-wheeler in the heavy traffic of the city is itself risky. How many times have I told you?"

She laughed.

"Once I complete my novel and become a celebrated author, I'll appoint you as my driver," she teased. "And then we will go like this." She imitated the movement of a snail with her fingers.

We laughed together. That was a peculiar quality of Teena. Nobody could be mad at her for long. She turned towards me and kissed me on my forehead. I continued with the hug that I had left midway. We remained entwined as she kept talking about her days without me, pausing periodically for my reactions. I enjoyed the sound of her voice as I keenly listened to her words. I realised how much I missed being with her as she brushed her fingers against my skin when she recollected the things she had kept aside to tell me when we met.

The sound of someone tapping on the glass woke me up. I looked at the empty space beside me that Teena had occupied a moment ago. Getting up from my bed, I quickly headed towards the window and saw the outline of a woman through the wet and blurred glass. I opened the window and Teena smiled at me.

"You could have kept the key here," she said.

"You wouldn't have woken me up then."

I hurried to the living room, took the key from the teapoy and turned it in the lock. Teena flew into my arms as soon as I opened the door. We stood cuddling each other for some time, unwilling to let go. The familiar scent of her body spray comforted me like a lost kid who found his way back home. She finally loosened her grip and held my hands.

"Feels like ages," I said.

"Same here," she said, tears showing up at the corner of her eyes.

"Come in," I said.

I took her bag from her and kept it inside before closing the door behind us.

"Did you fall from your scooter today?" I asked, remembering the prior conversation.

"No, you might have dreamt about it," she said.

Years of acquaintance with my mixing up of real and imaginary had made her regard my condition as something as normal as breathing. We did not bother about it much now. Even I stopped considering it as a problem that I had, rather, I accepted it as a part of my life.

"I'll take a quick shower," she said. "Please get me a cup of your strong coffee when I return."

CHAPTER 11

Teena was never fond of cooking whereas I took great pleasure in showing off my culinary skills when she was around. She looked more adorable to me today when she closed her eyes taking in the flavour of every spice in the *paneer* curry that I had prepared to eat with *chapati* for our breakfast. With half-open eyes, she signalled with her fingers that the food was delicious. There was a distinctive way in which my sensualist wife enjoyed everything. Her words and her countenance, when she explained what she felt, would make one want to experience them through her, in the same manner that she did. Because of this, I called her my John Keats.

I took a *chapati* from the casserole as she served me the curry. Since it had become a habit when I had my food alone, I unwittingly pressed the power button on the television remote control and tuned in to the news channel. Similar to the past five days, the channel exclusively discussed the indifference of the authorities as the reason for the lack of leads in the disappearance of the renowned author Rajagopal. Teena seized the remote from my hand and turned it off.

"I switch off my office phone when I come here and you're watching TV?" she asked crossly.

"I'm sorry, I didn't really mean to. It kind of became a routine," I apologised.

The hearty breakfast culminated with an apple pudding that I had made for her last evening. We savoured it slowly sitting on the wired chair in our small garden, listening to a bird as it whistled a melody. Teena then went to wash the dishes while I stood beside her so that I could spend more time with her when she was home.

We dusted our books together every Saturday morning. Malayalam and English books were kept on different shelves and novels, poetry and drama were allotted separate rows on each shelf. Once in a while, we also rearranged the order;

now they were organized according to the year of publication. Teena took out each book warily, giving special care to the edges while I wiped the dust with the clean cloth that we had maintained for the purpose.

At noon, we went out for lunch as usual. "This is the best part of the day," I would unfailingly say every time the car passed the gates into the broad outside world. It was after a whole week that the car and I were released from the curse of confinement at home. Teena always told me to try going out but I knew that it was better for someone like me to sit at home. There was also an inexplicable joy in waiting for the weekend so that Teena and I could go out together. Saturday was also the only day of the week that we did not care about what we ate. Flinging caution to the wind, we tried new delicacies, some of which we did not even know the names of.

A shopping followed the sumptuous lunch. We bought everything that I needed for a whole week. Teena had decided that our home required some more green companions. Thorough negotiations and discussions with the storekeeper and her own research on the internet brought her to the conclusion that she would buy a peace lily.

The ride back home was scenic. The midday temperature was subsiding. Tea plantations basked in the evening sun, making the view even prettier. Teena had her hand on my thigh as she took delight in the nature that she missed in the city. If not for her job, she would not have given up this paradise that she had adopted as her home.

Teena and I were taking out the shopping bags from the car when I suddenly remembered that I had not picked up the book that had been on my mind from the day the media started showing news of author Rajagopal. "What happened?" Teena asked. She proved yet again that she could easily read me; even the most subtle changes on my face would never go unnoticed by her eyes.

"I forgot to buy a book that I wanted so much to add to our collection!" I said. "Never mind, next week."

"Which one?" she asked.

"*Selvi* by Rajagopal. It's the last book that he wrote before he announced that he was taking a break from writing. Heard that it's also the author's favourite."

As soon as I told her about the book, Teena swiftly climbed the steps that led to the front door, opened it and proceeded straight to our room. I was startled and stood gaping at the direction in which she went. She soon returned with a naughty expression, holding something behind her. Coming closer, she revealed what was in her hand. An author-signed copy of the book *Selvi*.

To Teena,

Thanks for writing the book I couldn't write.

"Hey! That's amazing! You know him? What does this mean?"

"Thou shalt know when the time is ripe," she said, posing like a Shakespearean heroine. She grinned and touched the tip of my nose. "I want it to be a surprise. Wait for a few more months."

CHAPTER 12

Nabeesa, or Nabeesumma as we endearingly called her, was our only neighbour as there were no other houses in the region that we lived in. Nabeesumma's husband passed when she was forty, leaving her alone with three sons and a daughter, Naseema. Naseema was twelve when I first met her. Nabeesumma came to Munnar when one of her acquaintances arranged a job for her on a plantation. She sold her land in her village and bought the house so that she and her children could have the safety of a roof over their heads. "At least nobody will ask us to move out if we have a house of our own," Nabeesumma had once said to me. It was she who told me to call her *umma* and she had indeed been a mother to me.

Naseema was now the mother of the two-year-old Sulthana. Nabeesumma no longer toiled on the plantation since her sons and her son-in-law were well off with their restaurant business in Oman. They had also renovated the old house, erasing every trace of the poverty that they previously suffered from.

A visit to Nabeesumma's house was a part of our Sundays. As soon as Teena opened the gates, we heard Naseema call out, "*Umma*, they're here!" Nabeesumma looked up and grinned from ear to ear sitting in front of a bed of red chillies which she had scattered on a woven mat to dry in the sun. The red chillies on the mat and a saree-clad woman spreading them out with her hands evoked in me some forgotten memory or its fragments.

Sulthana was standing behind the front door peeking at us. "Baby! Come," Teena beckoned and opened her arms. Nabeesumma washed her hands, picked up the child and carried her on her hips. Teena and Nabeesumma struggled to get Sulthana to remember us but the weekly calls were apparently not enough for our faces to get imprinted inside her little brain. I sat down on a bench, entertained by the spectacle.

As the process went on, Naseema came with two glasses of steaming *sulaimani*, the spiced black tea, and a plate full of her sweet homemade snack, *neyyappam*. Teena gave up her attempt to befriend the child and sat down next to me. Nabeesumma handed over Sulthana to her mother and settled down on a plastic chair opposite us.

"How are things going, children?" she asked.

"Everything is good, *umma*," Teena said as she nibbled on her *neyyappam*.

"When are you coming to stay here? The poor boy is all alone. See, he has even lost some weight," she advocated for me as she did every time she saw us.

"Actually I am also dying to come and stay here," Teena said. "Let's see, I am positive that I will no longer have to depend on the job once I finish my novel."

"*Insha Allah*," she said, closing her eyes for a moment as if in silent prayer.

"And I have no worries about my hubby being alone here," Teena added, "as long as his mother lives just next door." She pinched

Nabeesumma lightly on the cheeks.

"This girl!" Nabeesumma creased her brows to fake anger and gave an affectionate slap on Teena's shoulder.

Walking out of Nabeesumma's home would mark the countdown of our time together. Neither Teena nor I would speak much after that. I dreaded this graveyard-like silence that swamped our home as the weekend came to a close. I also hated the knowledge that the same silence was to haunt me for the rest of the week.

Teena packed her things and set her alarm for three in the morning. "Why haven't you taken your meds?" she asked, picking up the white, round tablet that I had kept on top of the book *Selvi* that she gave me. I had placed the pill perfectly inside the moon on the cover of the book. Teena took my hand, placed the medicine inside my palm and poured me a glass of water from the jug. "Don't be careless with this, Roy," she said, looking upset.

Sitting on the bed, I mechanically swallowed the chemical that helped my brain sort out the world. I wanted to remain cheerful for the rest of the hours that she was going to be with me but I could never get over that unpleasant feeling inside my head. I sensed Teena's breath on the back of my neck and the touch of her fingers around my waist. Turning me around, she cupped my jaws with her hands and looked into my eyes. She then laid my face on her chest and gradually lowered herself onto the bed. I wanted to break down and cry but I did not. I had learnt to control my emotions from a very young age. We continued to hold on to each other while she ran her fingers through my hair, calming my nerves. At some point, I fell asleep.

Time, which had always been industrious and diligent since eternity, was not ready to compromise its reputation for two mere mortals. If it had a form, it would resemble an executioner wielding his axe and shrouded in black, who was trained to remain unmoved by the victim's emotions. If it was a temperature, it would probably be cold, not the pleasant cold of Munnar but the frosty cold of an Antarctic winter. Every human might have cursed it in vain at least once just as I did foolishly every Sunday night. The sudden startling sound of the alarm indicated that time had turned a blind eye to our aching hearts once again.

CHAPTER 13

After dropping Teena off at the bus station, I parked the car by the side of the road and slept for a while as I found it difficult to return to the solitude of the house that morning. The quietness inside the four walls would shout out her absence, reminding me how lonely I was without her. When I started back home, it was almost 7:30. A thin layer of fog still enveloped the atmosphere due to which I had to lean forward and concentrate hard to see what was ahead.

As I reached the gates of my house, I saw a white jeep with its rear side towards me parked inside. The word 'POLICE' written boldly in red colour became clearer as I neared it. I was unnerved, not only about why the police had appeared at my home but also about what I might have done to invite the presence of police there. I was not still sure about the characteristics of my illness, if or how this unnamed condition of mine would advance. Would I have unknowingly committed some crime and forgotten about it or taken it for a dream? Was somebody hurt because of me?

Two police officers, a male and a female, were asking something to Nabeesumma. Was she summoned? What was happening here? My hands shook as I turned the key off and got out of my car. The male officer walked towards me when he saw me standing there perplexed.

"Hi, I am sub inspector Asif. We came to see your wife, Teena. We couldn't reach her by phone during the weekend."

"She has the habit of switching off her office phone when she is on holiday. Please try calling her today." I checked my watch. "It's eight. She will switch it back on at around nine."

"Thank you," he said.

I stood watching the retreating figure of the police officer, deliberating whether to ask him why they wanted to see Teena. Was it not a basic courtesy on their part to tell me why they came asking for my wife? The officer halted and turned to me as if he heard my thoughts.

"Last week, two days before author Rajagopal was reported missing, Teena had posted a picture with him on Facebook. We just wanted to know if we could get some information from her."

I nodded. The police vehicle left at once and Nabeesumma went back after enquiring if I had something at home for my morning meal. I rushed in to jot down the incident in my journal which Teena had asked me to keep so that I could make a note of the real incidents and thereby sieve the truths from the mixture in my mind. This way I could prevent confusing people and getting myself confused when Teena was not with me. I opened my book and began to write.

18th August 2022: Police came

I stopped, took my phone, selected Nabeesumma's name from my contacts and touched the phone icon on its side. After a couple of rings, she answered.

"*Umma*, did the..., I mean, when did the police come?" I tactfully modified my sentence so as not to distress her. Though she had never acknowledged it, Nabeesumma was aware that I had a mental disorder. She never questioned me or Teena about it and had always pretended total ignorance. It was one of the best things about her; she never probed into others' affairs even when she was given the right to do so. "They came about ten minutes before you reached," she said. Yes, it had really happened. It was not a dream. It was not an illusion. The police were here. I pulled the book back towards me and completed the sentence.

18th August 2022: Police came looking for Teena to ask her about her picture with author Rajagopal.

My mobile sang the song that I had commissioned it to sing exclusively when my wife called. I picked up fast, having already started to miss that voice.

"Roy, I just reached," she said.

"How was the journey?" I asked.

"It was pretty much fine. I slept half of the time."

"Did you have your breakfast?"

"No, Saumya is preparing something. I doubt if she is experimenting with my stomach." She laughed.

"Ah, how's your roomie cousin? I forgot to ask," I said, reminding myself that I should tell her about the police before cutting the call.

"She's good, enjoying her singing lessons. Roy, do you have something to tell me?"

Like always, I felt good that she could sense it in my tone. "Yeah. The police came here. They asked for you."

"What for?"

"They were curious about the picture that you posted with author Rajagopal. They might want to know if you have something to tell them about him, you know, which would help them find him."

"Hmmm," she said.

"They will call you," I said.

"Okay."

"What happened? You sound dull."

"Nothing," she said. "I was just thinking about what you told me. Hey, I have got to go. There's going to be a lot of work today."

"Bye, Teena."

"Bye!" she said. "You should make some *dosas* for breakfast," she added. "There is enough batter in the fridge for two days."

"I will," I assured her.

"Bye, Roy"

"Bye."

Mondays had always been the worst days in the week for me ever since Teena got her job. After forcing myself to have my breakfast and cleaning the dishes and the kitchen sink, I searched for something that would distract me from the thoughts of Teena. *Selvi* could be a good friend to me, I decided. The book was small, something that could be read in a day. Like the other books of the literary wizard, the first sentence itself was arresting and hooked me into the universe that he had created with the magic of his fingers. I stretched my legs out onto the table and prepared myself to get immersed in the world of author

Rajagopal's words.

CHAPTER 14

I placed *Selvi* on the table, took out a tablet from the small, white plastic container and was preparing to pour water into the glass from the jug when Teena called. I kept the medicine on top of the book and attended the call, relaxing myself on the bed.

"Had oats for supper, didn't you?" she asked before I even said the opening 'hello'.

"No, a mouth-watering fish curry and rice *pathiri*," I proudly declared.

"Wow! Nabeesumma, for sure," she said. "She knows that you are reluctant to cook on the day I go back after my leave."

I chuckled. "It's not like that," I said. "It was not necessary to cook after morning today. Some food is remaining there in the fridge. Did you eat?"

"Yeah, Saumya had everything ready by the time I returned from the office. Roy, I'll be sleeping early today. A heavy headache. I'll call you tomorrow morning."

"What happened?" I asked, panic rising from inside my chest.

"It's nothing. I had to spend a lot of time staring at the laptop screen today. Don't worry, I just need a good night's sleep."

"Take care then. Sleep well."

"You too," she said.

I kept my phone on the table and pulled up the blanket over me. Proper sleep was also prescribed to me to help me lead a somewhat normal life. My eyelids felt heavy and droopy as soon as my head touched the pillow and I realised how tired I was. Stretching out my hand, I turned off the table lamp, arranging the perfect environment for a perfect sleep.

I was awakened by a series of banging on the glass. Though the bright beam of the full moon was efficiently lighting up the room, I turned on the table lamp before I got out of bed. The transparent curtains revealed the silhouette of someone standing outside. Drawing them back, I opened the window.

A girl, probably in her late teens, stood alone staring at me unblinkingly. The light lavished on the land by the moon illuminated her well. She was dressed in the traditional Tamil attire of *pavada* and *dhavani*, yellow in colour but faded due to its oldness. A long beaded necklace hung around her neck, its pendent hidden by the folds of her *dhavani*. Her hair was tightly braided and it resembled the hairstyle of a Tamil village girl of a bygone era. It was also decorated with a rose which had already started wilting. The excessive oil on her hair seemed to have seeped onto her face, making her dusky skin even duskier. Her wrists were covered with red glass bangles and a small red *bindi* adorned her forehead. On her ears shone a pair of small studs and a nose pin that matched it was worn on her nose. As I stood observing her, she started to speak.

"Shall I tell you where the missing ones are?"

I kept looking at her clueless.

"On the way from Vazhikkadavu to Nadukani, towards the left, there is Maruthanpuzha," she continued without waiting for my response, "From Maruthanpuzha, on the way to Chinnathodu, after the check post, there is a big board with a picture of an elephant on it. Go right, and there is a route to the forest where you will find an old house. The missing ones are there."

My eyes remained glued to her face for some more time. Who was she? Why did she tell me this now? What was it that she wanted from me? I turned and glanced at the book and my neglected pill on it about which I had totally forgotten when Teena's call came. The cover of *Selvi* resembled what I saw outside when I opened my window. I then turned back to look at the girl again. She was, however, away from my window, going out of my home, moving gracefully like a *Yakshi*, the female mythological spirit, whom I had seen in old Malayalam movies. I watched her as she walked without looking back and slowly faded into the shadows.

Before I knew it, I had picked up my phone and started calling Teena. I sat listening to her caller tune for quite some time before it ended and she spoke. "Hello, Roy," she said, her voice gruff from sleepiness. "Teena, shall I tell you where the missing ones are?" I asked. "Mm," she mumbled. "On the way from Vazhikkadavu to Nadukani, towards the left, there is Maruthanpuzha. From Maruthanpuzha, on the way to Chinnathodu, after the check post, there is a big board with a picture of an elephant on it. Go right, and there is a route to the forest where you will find an old house. The missing ones are there," I said, repeating every word of the girl as if in a trance. There was a brief pause from the other side. "Must be a dream, Roy," Teena replied drowsily. "Take your meds and sleep. Okay? Goodnight."

CHAPTER 15

The cornflakes drowned in the milk that I had generously poured into the bowl. I was too lazy to prepare something for breakfast today. Moreover, I woke up only at nine-thirty when Teena called me before she started for her office. Taking the bowl in one hand and *Selvi* in the other, I settled down on the sofa. The dining table was not a necessity to me and the one that was in the room was bought upon the insistence of Teena. I mindlessly had my food while my concentration was completely on the book.

My phone rang from the kitchen. I might have absent-mindedly placed it on the kitchen slab. The bright light from its screen glowed in the darkness of the room which made it easy for me to locate it.

"Hello, Teena."

"Roy, were you running?"

"The phone was in the kitchen. By the way, you don't usually call me during these hours. What happened?"

"Didn't you tell me the names of some places yesterday night?"

I could not recollect calling her yesterday after she said she was going to sleep. "You said you were going to sleep early."

"Yes, but you called me in the middle of the night. At around 12. Don't you remember? And you told me about some route."

A vague image of a girl came to my memory. "I remember seeing a girl outside our window. She spoke to me. But it was a dream."

"Umm… One of the places that you mentioned was Vazhikkadavu. Can you recall something now?"

"I now remember calling you. But I can't recollect anything that I said. I took my medicine and went to sleep just as you told me.

I had a sound sleep after that. I'm sorry."

"It's fine, Roy. Text me if something comes to your mind. I'll call you at lunchtime. Bye."

"Bye."

I went to the bedroom and checked my diary to see if I had written down anything about what the girl told me. Nothing was mentioned there. Teena had told me it was a dream and I might have left it at that. Why did she want to know about my dream? Why did something from my unreal universe become important to her? I made a mental note to ask her the next time we spoke.

It was dark outside even though it was time for the day to shine bright. I opened the windows and saw that the sky had put on a grey apparel. The clouds were pregnant with rain and there were distant rumblings of thunder that confirmed their expectancy. For me, it was the time to read. The music played on the leaves by the showers and the fragrance that emanated from the soil on the first touch of rain would invariably enhance my reading experience. I needed to finish all my work before the rain started to pour down so that I could come and relax on the sofa with the book.

I prepared a quick lunch of easy vegetable fried rice with whatever there was inside the refrigerator. Rajagopal had framed his plot in such a way that his readers would not be able to keep the book down until they finished reading it. I was so absorbed in the book that I had to tear my eyes from it to do the mandatory domestic chores. While I was waiting for the rice to get cooked, the name 'Teena Personal' flashed on my mobile phone screen.

"Hey, calling on Tuesday from your personal number. I smell a trip."

"Yeah, your dream gave me some hints about where author Rajagopal might be. I am planning on an investigation."

"It has been some time since you went behind your crazy, wild thoughts," I remarked just to tease her.

"You're right," she said, laughing. "It has indeed been a while."

"When are you going?"

"I'm already at the bus stop. The bus will arrive soon."

"So you've already set out? How is your headache?"

"That's long gone. I'm alright now. The bus has come. I'll call you. Bye!"

"Hey, where…"

I forgot to ask her where she was going. Neither did I ask her what was the clue that she got from my dream. She asked me about a location when she called me before. I tried hard to remember it but I could not. She might have gone there. I texted her where she was going but the message did not get delivered. A heavy rain started all of a sudden and its song reverberated all around. I went inside the kitchen to check on my rice.

CHAPTER 16

The car and I never stepped out of the gates without Teena, and after such a long time, it felt uncomfortable to be out alone, like being in the middle of the road with no clothes on. Insecurity kicked in as I drove inside the parking area of the police station where uniformed and non-uniformed humans were running around like actors in a play with varied expressions on their faces. A drop of sweat trickled down my face because of my social anxiety even though the morning was cold as usual. I realised what years of isolation could do to a person.

I parked the car by the side of a tree and headed inside. The situation indoors terrified me even more. There were constant opening and closing of doors and officers could be seen moving quickly about as if they were teleporting from the door to their destination. Some were fixed on their seats and had their necks leaned towards the computer monitors in front of them. People like me were watching the whole scene, waiting to talk to the first person who would be kind enough not to pretend that we were invisible.

I did not know whom to approach with my problem. Licking my dry lips, I tried to grab the attention of someone there, looking from one to the next. As I stood there watching the officers, I saw three of them staring at me and talking among themselves. One of them, the sub-inspector who came the other day asking for Teena, quickly walked towards me.

"You're Teena's husband, aren't you?" he asked.

"Yes," I said, nervously.

"What happened? Why are you here?"

"I-I came to file a complaint."

"Well, tell me." He looked steadily into my eyes.

"T-Teena is missing from yesterday noon," I

stammered.

"Oh, you wait here," he said and hurried into a room.

I stood there taking deep breaths to compose myself. Soon, I was summoned into the circle inspector's office. In contrast to the chaotic and suffocating atmosphere outside, the CI's room was rather placid as if the noise itself chose to maintain discipline in front of the superior officer. The CI was sitting behind his desk busily writing something while the SI stood beside him looking at me. The law and order of the locality were stacked as files in front of the CI and several successful and closed cases rested inside two big shelves by the side of the desk. A thick layer of dust could be spotted on the white dial-pad of the landphone kept close to his left hand as well as on the three trophies and on the decorative piece which held two miniature metal Indian national flags. The white wall had three things on it – a picture of Mahatma Gandhi, a calendar on which again there was Gandhiji and the words 'KERALA GOVERNMENT' written in both Malayalam and English and a large wooden board with the names of the CIs who had worked in the station from

1993 to the present. The last among the names was Ajith Ishwar.

"Please," said the CI motioning towards the empty chairs in front of him. I sat there anxiously twisting my fingers, expecting him to ask me something. "Your wife works at Ernakulam, right? Why do you feel she is missing?" he asked. "I can't reach her," I said raising my mobile phone. "She told me she was going on a trip. Her phone is switched off now." I somehow completed my statements in spite of my shivering voice. "Do you have the contact number of anyone else travelling with her?" he enquired unsympathetically. "She has gone alone," I said. "Did you ask anyone else? Friends or colleagues or someone like that?" he continued as though he was following a format. "There's no use," I said. "Nobody knows." The CI glanced at the SI, a tint of annoyance visible in his eyes. "It has not been 24 hours since you stopped hearing from your wife. Do we need to consider someone missing before that? What if she ran out of batteries?" He looked at me like I was a child who was throwing unnecessary tantrums at a bakery. "She would have called me no matter what. Something has happened to her," I insisted. "Please calm down," he said. "Okay, do one thing. Lodge a complaint and we will look into the matter."

I walked uncertainly out of the room, went to the writer and gave my official complaint. She wrote down everything that I narrated to her and passed the paper to me for my signature. I read it again to make sure that nothing was left out, signed the paper and gave it back. I then immediately went back inside the CI's room.

The two policemen seemed surprised to see me there for a second time. "Haven't you given the complaint?" the SI asked me. "Yes," I said. "Haven't you written down your contact number?" he asked. "Yes," I said. "Fine. We'll inquire and let you know," the CI said as he got up and started to move towards the door held open by the SI. "Aren't you going to investigate now?" I asked. The vexed CI looked at the SI who began to soothingly explain the procedures to me. "See, each case has its own mode of investigation. We'll ask the cyber department to trace her location. We can find her easily." He gently tried to guide me out of the room but I was unyielding. This was just another case to them but for me, Teena was my life. "It has been more than a week since author Rajagopal went missing. You couldn't find him. What if the same happens to Teena? What if you won't be able to find her if you use your ordinary procedure? Moreover, she has gone in search of Rajagopal." The CI creased his brows and looked distrustfully at me. "How do you know that?" he asked. "I gave her the hint on his whereabouts," I said. The CI looked at me more suspiciously. "So you know where author Rajagopal is?" he asked. I did not think about what I was saying. I had no idea how I would respond to such follow-up questions. "It was a-a dream," I stammered, wiping my sweat with a handkerchief. "I t-told her about it from a dream. But I forgot what I told her."

CHAPTER 17

Anybody who would have listened to me that day would have concluded that I was crazy. I could not blame them. What else were they supposed to feel when someone came and told them that he received information about a place from his dream and that his wife had gone following the route from that dream? The CI walked past me angrily closely followed by the SI. I went back to the car and took out *Selvi*. A strange confidence embraced me when I held on to the book.

I remained seated on a chair next to the door and refused to return home as I felt that the police had not taken my case seriously. I wanted to make sure that they would start their search for Teena before something bad happened. It was three in the afternoon when the white jeep finally came back to the station.

"When did you come?" the CI asked me.

"I did not leave."

"Roy!" he began, trying to bring some compassion into his voice. "The police called up Teena's colleagues and her roommate. They all are sure that she is still on her trip. They told us that it is not uncommon for her to switch off her mobile phone and vanish like this. There is not even a slight chance of any mishap. Let's wait for a day or two and see if she comes back."

Things went beyond my tolerance level. I scurried after the CI as he walked inside and said in a raised voice. "You've got nothing to lose if something happens to her. Why can't you believe me when I say that she is in danger?" The CI stopped in his tracks and turned towards me. "Don't test my patience," he said. "I came to know that you are unwell and that's the only reason why I don't kick you out. Now, please go home and let us do what we can." "She went looking for author Rajagopal," I repeated. "Your wife told us that she is not acquainted with Rajagopal and that she got the picture when she unexpectedly saw him at a café," he said, his voice revealing the rage boiling within him, threatening to erupt any time. I opened the book in my hand and turned to the page where the author had written his note for Teena. "See this," I said. "Would he write this for a random fan he met at a coffee shop?"

The officers stared at the words in the book. *Thanks for writing the book I couldn't write.* With an exasperated expression on his face, the CI told me, "It was *your wife* who told us that she didn't know Rajagopal. Why did she lie to us?" I remained mute. I had no answer to give the policeman. "Roy," he said as he put his hand on my shoulder, "Let me tell you some of my thoughts. Teena is beautiful, creative and thoroughly active on social media. She will have a lot of friends, won't she? Above all, she's way too young for you." "Sir," the SI attempted to cut in but the CI waved him off. I was desperately trying to prevent his words from entering my head. Even though I was aware that Teena would have had a better life if I had not crossed her path on that fateful day, I was completely confident that she had not left me. She was not a coward who would lie to me and run away. If she was leaving, she would have told me and I would never have stopped her from doing what she desired even if it hurt me. I was not concerned about my life. I was only scared of my condition. If my brain tricked me into believing the officer's words, I would stop my search for Teena and there would be no one to rescue her. All I wanted was to know that she was safe. The CI mercilessly continued, "I don't find any compatible factors between you both. You don't live together, neither do you have any kids. Just think about it, what if she no longer wants to live with you? Have you seen her recent Facebook post, the one she posted just before she left?" I shook my head. He took out his mobile phone from the side pocket of his pants, opened the app, typed Teena's name on the search bar and showed it to me. "See, 'Going on a solo trip chasing a dream. All credit to my husband'. What does that mean?" He paused and said, "We can't do anything about a woman who has left her husband."

I looked at him fighting back my tears and wrath and stepped out of the station without uttering another word. A great effort was needed for me even to make the smallest movement. My body ached each time I raised my leg to move forward. The CI's words echoed inside my head. I repeatedly told myself that I had to save Teena and tried to put in a conscious effort to forget everything else.

I turned the key, opened the door and sat inside my car. I felt a lump in my throat but for some reason, I could not cry. As I wanted to get out of the premises quickly, I turned on the ignition and drove out of the gates. I had no sense of direction or destination. Driving straight, I sped past the plantations, the silver oaks and the little shops by the road until I reached a deserted, uninhabited and isolated place. I pulled over behind a tree where I would not be easily spotted and rested my head on the steering wheel. Stress and sorrow took over me. Fatigue crept into my body starting from my legs, slowly advancing into my hands and then to my head. It became increasingly tough for me to keep my eyes open. Sleep came to my aid when tears failed.

CHAPTER 18

It was dark and cold when I woke up. I might have slept for too long. A streetlight glowed brightly above and tiny droplets of water could be seen on the windscreen. I wondered why I did not hear the pitter-patter of rain on the roof. As I prepared to start for home, a headlight from a car coming from the opposite direction shone on my face and I shielded my eyes with my hands. The vehicle braked in front of my car and Ashwathy, Teena's friend, alighted from it and waved at me. I opened the door and walked towards her.

"What are you doing here alone?" she asked.

"Teena's phone is switched off," I said. "I am sure something unfortunate has happened. I went to the police but they took me for a madman and..."

"Come with me. Let's go to my flat and talk."

I locked my car and went with Ashwathy to her apartment. My shattered mind needed someone to talk to. I knew that Teena would never leave me but the police officer's words did play their part in messing up my thoughts. During the drive, I briefed Ashwathy about what Teena told me about her trip and what happened at the station. She listened without interrupting as I opened up to her.

We reached Ashwathy's flat in less than half an hour. She parked her car in her parking area and led me inside the building. Teena and I were not aware that she lived so close by. Had we known, we would definitely have visited earlier. We entered the lift and she pressed the number '5'.

The doors of the lift opened right in front of '5F' where Ashwathy lived. She clicked the locks open and switched on the lights before inviting me inside. The room spoke for itself that the occupant lived alone. There was minimal furniture in the living cum dining room among which was an old dining table that rested at its far end, near the kitchen. "I'll get you a cup of coffee," she said as she gestured for me to sit.

"Roy!" she called out from the kitchen.

"Mm?" I raised my head.

"Did you really believe the things that the police told you?"

"I didn't. But when the officer told me all that, I..."

"They don't know anything about you, do they? Roy, you know about your relationship. You know about Teena. She chose you even when she knew that her family would renounce her for her choice. She is someone who decided to be alone just to live with you. She's impulsive but do you think it was only a spur-of-the-moment decision for her? No! She knew that it was you whom she wanted to spend the rest of her life with."

"I know, but..."

Ashwathy brought two cups of coffee and placed them on the dining table. "Aren't you ashamed to sit here like this because of something someone told you calculatedly to break you?" she asked, her fury starting to be decipherable in her voice. "If Teena comes to know of this…"

"I didn't believe anything he said, trust me," I protested. "Ashwathy, nobody else will understand Teena and me and our bond. People will only think why Teena, who could have easily found a better partner, be with a mentally ill person."

"Please come out of your unnecessary inferiority complex," she advised. "Teena is certain that there are some truths and prophecies in your dreams. She has told me that your dreams are a gift. That's precisely why she went in search of Rajagopal."

Ashwathy was right. I knew that Teena never regretted her decision to marry me. She loved me more than anything else. She wanted to resign from her job and come and live with me as soon as her novel was published. Only Ashwathy knew the profundity of Teena's feelings for me. No one else had any right to comment on our life.

Only one thing disturbed me on my way back as I sat in Ashwathy's car. "No matter how much I try, I can't remember the names of the locations that I mentioned to Teena," I told Ashwathy. "You should somehow find them, Roy. Keep on thinking and they'll come to you," she replied. "You should take this as a challenge," she continued, "and find her without any help. You must emerge victorious in front of people who insulted you. It is your responsibility. Only you can save her, Roy. Only you."

It was then that I realised that we were not going to the place where my car was parked. I looked quizzically at her. "To CI Ajith Ishwar's house," she said. "You have something to tell him, don't you?" Ashwathy parked in front of a pair of large wooden gates. "Go ahead," she said.

I got out of the car, confidently opened the gates and marched towards the palatial house. The ornate lights outside were intense enough to let one see the wide premises clearly. My footsteps could be heard distinctly on the tiled floor due to the silence of the night. I reached his doorstep and pressed the bell. The CI opened the door.

"I just came to inform you one thing. The depth of our love is not something a cold-hearted policeman like you can fathom. It is much beyond your comprehension. Teena would never leave me. I want you to know that your words have only encouraged me to search for my wife on my own. I will find my Teena."

PART 3

**August 20, 2022 to
August 26, 2022**

CHAPTER 19

Sub-inspector Asif stood watching as Roy drove off from the police station in his car. He felt sorry for the devastated man. Were they, the people-friendly *janamaithri* police, supposed to say such cruel words to a civilian who came to them seeking help to find his missing wife? According to the protocol, he was supposed to put up with everything that his superiors did. Still, as a human being, he could not help pointing out, in the humblest way possible, the heartlessness of what CI Ajith Ishwar just did. No wonder his colleagues called him an emotional fool behind his back.

"Sir, that was a bit too much," he said.

"I did it on purpose," Ajith replied. "I need you to keep a close watch on him. He should be on our suspects' list till we can prove that he has got nothing to do with the disappearance of author Rajagopal and Teena."

"I think he is innocent, sir."

"That's because you are too naïve. She herself has written 'All credit to my husband'. There's something fishy about that. Let's see. And," Ajith added, "I want to know everything about Roy, apart from the fact that he is a sick man living alone with occasional visits from his wife."

Roy's statement that the police had nothing to lose if something happened to his wife provoked Ajith. He had started to become sensitive towards Roy and the case when he came to know about the complainant's condition but his irate words made Ajith turn against him. "Asif," he called as the SI was about to go to his room. "Did you check Teena's phone location?"

"Yes sir, before getting switched off, it was in Mayyanthani tower area," Asif responded.

"Track it as soon as she switches it on," Ajith ordered.

"Sure sir. I will deal with this case. I thought Teena's missing would be linked to Rajagopal's. That's why I took it to you. I'm sorry, sir."

"You don't have to rule out such a possibility till we find at least one of them," Ajith said. "What if they are together?"

Asif reached his room and turned on his computer. He noticed that his keyboard and monitor were completely covered in dust. He thought of the irresponsibility of the cleaning lady who had no respect for her job. Being a drama queen, she had made the staff believe that she was too unwell to do strenuous work. Despite becoming a laughing stock for his humanity, he was not stupid enough to trust her. Neither did he tip her like the others, not even a rupee.

The old computer leisurely took a complete three minutes to boot up. Asif waited another minute before he logged in to his Facebook account. Even though he had seen Teena's picture, he had never checked her Facebook profile. He typed in the name 'Teena' on his search bar only to find that there were too many of them. He then tried adding Roy to her name, although he did not think that someone like Teena would change her surname after marriage. However, making him understand again that he was always too quick to judge, Teena's face appeared as the first result on his computer screen. He clicked on the profile and viewed her account. The most recent post in it, which could be spotted at once, was *'Going on a solo trip chasing a dream. All credit to my husband,'* the one that made CI Ajith suspicious about her husband's role in her disappearance. Scrolling down the comments, he stopped when he found one that was catchy.

Dr Ashwathy Rajan

Pack your bags and come. I'm waiting!

Asif clicked on Dr Ashwathy Rajan's profile and checked for the name of the hospital in which she worked. WYW hospital, New Delhi. He opened a new tab and copied and pasted the name of the hospital on the browser. He further clicked on the hospital's website and dialled Ashwathy's number from it.

"Hello!" Ashwathy's voice sounded as if she was in haste.

"Hello, is this Dr Ashwathy Rajan?"

"Yes."

"I'm sub-inspector Asif. I want to inquire about Teena Roy. Her husband Roy has given a complaint that she is missing."

"Wait," she said. There was a long silence before she spoke again. "Tell me, what happened?"

"As I said, Teena's husband Roy has given us a complaint that Teena is missing. I was scrolling through the comments of her last Facebook post and found that you had invited her to come and stay with you."

"I just thought it was one of her usual trips when I commented," she said.

"We talked to one of her colleagues and her roommate. They told us that she has this habit of going on solo trips. Everybody believes that she will return on her own. But her husband is sure that something has gone wrong," explained Asif.

"If Roy says so, you must take it seriously," she said. "I have known them personally for many years. Nobody can even guess the level of emotional bonding that they have."

CHAPTER 20

The day at *Vibes Today* had not begun. Roy reached there at nine in the morning and sat on the steps that led to the office. The traffic was already at its peak and angry horns blared all around. He had bought the morning paper from a tea shop where he stopped to have some tea to ward off his exhaustion from the four-hour drive. He scrutinised the newspaper to check if there was any information about a missing woman or author Rajagopal. The print media seemed to have decided to push author Rajagopal to the background and replace its pages with fresh and appealing topics. Nothing in this world remained news for long. As far as the populace was concerned, they wanted new things every other day to discuss within their social groups without getting bored. With dread in his heart, he looked for news of unidentified corpses and was relieved that there were none. While he was sitting there going through the paper, the first employee arrived.

Tony had not expected to see Teena's husband in front of his office, blocking his way. He was already feeling guilty when the police called him the previous day to ask him if he believed that his co-worker Teena was missing. Teena had picked up her things and left after he casually remarked that his friend saw author Rajagopal inside a bus that went to Vazhikkadavu. Seeing the glow in her eyes when he mentioned the name of the place, Tony was taken aback. He sat watching nervously as Teena made a quick phone call and then scribbled in her notepad after looking up something in Google Maps. If she had gone in search of the missing author, he knew that it was because of him, but he was too scared to let the police know about this. He feared that he would be dragged into this case and even taken to the police station to be questioned. He had a hope that Teena might have returned the previous night. The unexpected appearance of Roy at his workplace confirmed that she had neither returned nor called.

Roy recognised Tony as soon as he removed his helmet. His eyes gave the impression that he was trying to hide something from Roy, as if all he wanted was to run away. However, Tony smiled and shook hands with Roy and asked him if Teena was back yet.

"No," said Roy. "That's why I am here. I need to know some things."

"The manager will be here soon. You can wait inside," Tony replied, tactfully preventing Roy from asking him anything.

Roy walked inside the office with Tony. The small lobby had only a black leather three-seater sofa and a wooden teapoy. He sat on the sofa looking outside at the road through the transparent glass windows. Drivers, probably on their way to work, competed to get to the front in the two-lane pathway. Bikes sped through the footpath, almost knocking down the pedestrians. A car just missed crashing into another by a hair's breadth. Roy wondered how Teena survived amidst this hustle and bustle. He took out his phone and tried calling her number the third time that day. He listened to it expectantly before disappointment crept into his eyes and he placed his phone back inside his shirt pocket.

The manager pushed open the door suddenly and was startled to see someone sitting on the sofa. He eyed the man suspiciously as he walked in. Roy stood up to greet the manager but he walked past quickly as a flash. Roy was fed up with people ignoring him when he was in a situation like this. After sitting there for some more time, he was summoned to the manager's room.

"Good morning, Roy," the manager said.

"Good morning."

"I'm sorry I didn't recognise you. Tony said you had something to ask me. Go on," he said without beating around the bush.

"Teena spends most of her time here," Roy began, his uneasiness and sorrow starting to show in his voice. "She has been gone for almost two days now. Why didn't you do anything about it?"

"See Roy, this is not the first time that she has gone like this." The manager took a deep breath, trying to control his anger. "There is no need to worry. I'm sure she will call you very soon."

"Her mobile phone is still switched off. The last time she called, she informed me that she was going after author Rajagopal. Can you give me any information regarding that?"

The door opened and Tony came in with some papers in his hand. The manager signalled him to wait. Tony's heavy heart did not allow him to peacefully do his job. He could not help but pop in and listen to their conversation. He was confused about whether he should confess his part in Teena's decision to go after the missing author or keep his mouth shut and pretend like nothing happened.

"I'm sorry but I can't help you with the matter," the manager replied. "She does not have the habit of sharing her plans with anybody. Teena is a smart woman, Roy. She can take care of herself. You know that it is her habit to go on occasional expeditions like this, don't you? Stay calm and wait for her call. Everything's going to be okay."

CHAPTER 21

Ajith puffed out a cloud of smoke standing on the balcony of his apartment. He enjoyed watching it as he released it slowly from his mouth till it blended with the other pollutants in the atmosphere. Despite being warned that his habit of smoking was taking its toll on his health, he could not get over the practice of lighting a cigarette after food. He justified himself by thinking that everything around him, including the air that he breathed and the food that he consumed, was contaminated. However, today he used tobacco not only as a habit but also as a means to find peace when his job became tougher than ever. He opened his WhatsApp on his mobile phone and replayed the voice message of circle-inspector Suresh who worked at Ernakulam and had been his friend from the day they joined their police training together. Ajith had sent Teena's picture with Rajagopal to Suresh and had asked him to find out the location in which it was taken.

I knew that the picture was taken at a café that I had once visited. I just wanted to make sure before informing you. It is owned by a man named Deepak. The building functions as a publishing house, a café and a library. If you want I'll talk to him officially and let you know. Since Rajagopal had written a note like that for Teena, I feel that the cases are connected.

I'll tell you. Ajith typed back. He still could not believe that Teena was missing. Like everyone else, he thought that she was going return soon and that it would be foolish to go after her and waste their time when they had other pressing matters to attend to. On the other hand, he also feared that if something happened to her, the public would take up the matter and criticize the whole department for their negligence. CI Ajith Ishwar was known for his efficiency in dealing with the toughest of situations. Being left amidst such a dilemma in which he was unsure if he should consider Roy's complaint or not, he dreaded that the case was going to be the end of all his good reputations.

Ajith got inside the jeep without making his driver wait for him. He considered time to be very precious, so much so that he had made it his principle not to waste anybody's time. His irritable mood, however, was going to spare none. He glared at the others on the road for their slightest mistakes, most of which he would not have noticed on other days. Two young men were shouted at by the CI for going too slow and not giving way to his jeep. The poor driver also received a good amount of scolding for accidentally hitting a small pothole.

SI Asif was waiting for him when he reached the police station. "What is it going to be!" Ajith mumbled to himself as he pushed open the door and entered his room. He could not handle any more trouble; not today, not in any of the coming days.

Asif stood hesitantly as he could sense that his superior officer was in a foul mood. He knew that it would be unwise to talk to Ajith now. The man was notorious for his temper among the people who worked under him. Nevertheless, Asif did not have any other choice but to show Ajith what he found. He decided to wait till the officer settled down and was approachable enough.

"Sir, please take a look at this," Asif said, tentatively showing his mobile phone screen to Ajith after standing there for five minutes. Ajith took the phone from him and observed that the screen showed the Facebook profile of Deepak, the publishing house owner that Suresh told him about. Deepak had named his profile 'Deepak Booksthakam'.

"How did you reach his profile?" Ajith asked, impressed with the skills of the SI.

"I found a picture of this man, his name is Deepak, and Teena together on Teena's Facebook page and I noticed that the picture had the same background as the other picture; the one which made us curious about Teena's relationship with Rajagopal. So, I searched the internet for the location and came to know that it is a café owned by Deepak," Asif replied.

"I have to accept that you are brilliant, Asif. I had asked Suresh for help and he told me the name of the place this morning. Well, good work."

"Thank you, sir."

"I'll ask Suresh to officially question him. We can't be away from here right now. Did you get any more information about Roy?"

"I'm afraid I haven't got anything useful, sir. There is a woman who stays near Roy's house but she doesn't know anything beyond what we already know. Ah, she said that his native place is somewhere in Alappuzha and that he had a failed marriage before he married Teena."

"What if his first wife left him when she came to know that he was mentally unstable, or perhaps even a threat to her life?"

Asif didn't say anything. He understood that Ajith was deeply prejudiced about Roy. Consciously or unconsciously, Ajith was convinced that Roy had some part to play in the case if Teena was indeed missing. Asif knew that it would not do him any good if he voiced his opinion, rather, it might make him fall out of the CI's favour.

Ajith took his phone from his table and messaged Suresh that he needed his assistance again. *Please talk to Deepak like you said. He might give us some vital information about the missing cases.* He further leaned back on his chair contemplating how to go on with the investigation. It would be fortunate, he thought, if Teena had really gone in search of author Rajagopal and Deepak knew about it. Ajith wished that Teena would return that night with a clear idea about where Rajagopal was and would lead the police there, thereby taking the weight off his chest. Little did he know that the surprise that awaited him was much more than what he imagined.

CHAPTER 22

Roy got up after having a scanty lunch at a roadside restaurant. He had not eaten anything else that day since he was in a hurry to reach Teena's office. The indifferent attitude of the manager disappointed Roy. It confirmed his belief that every staff in an establishment was easily replaceable. He felt that no other soul cared about what happened to Teena.

Roy's next plan was to meet Deepak. He typed the name 'Booksthakam' in Google Maps and kept his phone on the passenger seat after turning the volume up. The traffic in the city was no better even during non-office hours and the afternoon sun was beating down brutally. The combination of the two was unbearable for Roy who was accustomed to the empty roads and the much-endurable heat of a hill station. The heat was forcing its way inside as if it was poking fun at the air conditioner. The meal, the temperature and the smell of the closed vehicle made him nauseous.

After a tedious drive, Roy reached the building that housed the café. He saw a large board 'Booksthakam' with an arrow pointed towards the top. Climbing the flight of stairs that led to the café, Roy hoped that Deepak would believe him and help him with his investigation. After all, he was not just Teena's publisher but a trusted friend too.

Deepak was truly surprised when he saw Roy walking towards him just some minutes after the police called him to inquire about Teena and Rajagopal. Words were not needed to understand the man's grief and distress; his face itself narrated the pangs of his soul which convinced Deepak that the officer's words were true. Roy did believe that his wife was missing. Sitting opposite Deepak, Roy stared at him like it was difficult to initiate a conversation.

"Any news about Teena?" Deepak asked to break the ice. "No," Roy said. Both of them remained silent for a moment before Roy spoke again. "I went to her office but they did not provide me with any useful information either." "We will find her, Roy. No matter where she is." Deepak was ashamed at his own insincere words. He knew that such were the words that were used when the speaker had nothing to offer other than those meaningless remarks which were meant more to console the speaker that he had done something. "Don't get tensed," he added.

Roy ignored Deepak's statements. It was not mere comfort that he wanted. He wanted some practical help, a clue that would lead him to Teena. "Don't you find anything strange about Teena disappearing after just seven days of Rajagopal's missing? As if they both are targeted by the same person? Deepak remained quiet and Roy continued. "Why did Teena say she was not acquainted with Rajagopal? Do you know Rajagopal?" Deepak started to get nervous just like every time he was forced to lie. "Only like you know him, through his books," he managed to say. "You're making a mountain out of a molehill, Roy. She'll come back."

Deepak's phone rang and he thanked the

heavens for blessing him with an opportunity to escape sitting face-to-face with Roy. He excused himself and went outside with his mobile phone. It was only when he closed the door behind him that he felt like checking the name of the caller. Tony Vibes Today. Why was Teena's colleague calling him? He picked up the call before it stopped ringing.

"Hello, Tony," he said.

"Deepak, I need to say this to someone. Just before Rajagopal was reported missing, one of my friends saw him on Vazhikkadavu bus. I told this to Teena one day and it was that afternoon that she went on her trip," Tony poured out as though he wanted to get it out of his mind as soon as possible.

"So Teena would have gone looking for Rajagopal," Deepak responded after thinking for a few seconds.

"Teena's husband was here in the morning. He questioned the manager about why none of us were bothered about Teena's missing." Tony said, on the verge of panicking.

"He's here. Don't worry. Let me talk to him."

Deepak walked back inside concocting plans to make Roy leave his office peacefully. Even though the police enquiry and Tony's panicky phone call succeeded in planting the seed of suspicion in him as well about Teena's safety, he did not want Roy to know that he suspected Teena to be in danger. However, he was startled to see Roy standing near the bookshelf behind his chair and holding the book '*Selvi*' in his hand; Deepak's personal copy with the author's signature and the note, '*To Deepak, with love Rajagopal*'. Roy lifted his head glowering at Deepak. The expression in Roy's eyes sent shivers down his spine and he started his explanation without even an opening apology. "Teena introduced him to me. Her novel is based on Rajagopal's life. It was when she nearly completed it that Rajagopal went missing." Roy looked at him, his expression inscrutable. "Come with me," he said. Deepak followed him as he descended the steps, without having any idea where he was taking him. "Teena and I had signed a contract with Rajagopal that we will keep the matter confidential till the book comes out. That's why Teena lied to the police," Deepak continued. Roy quickened his pace and got inside his car with Deepak at his heels. "Teena wished to complete her novel, quit her job and come and live with you. As for me, I have borrowed some money to set up my business. So we desperately needed Rajagopal to come back. She might have thought that she could bring him back and finish her manuscript." "Show me the way to Teena's apartment," Roy commanded.

Both of them did not speak another word about Teena during the drive. Deepak was scared of the person Roy had become when he came to know that Deepak had lied to him. He did not even dare to look at Roy's face, let alone say sorry.

Soumya's mellifluous music greeted them as they moved towards the door of her apartment. The song stopped abruptly as the calling bell sounded and she opened the door without any delay. "Hi," she said, smiling at them. The pleasant faces of Teena's acquaintances enraged Roy as he felt that they were unconcerned about her. "Where's Teena's room?" he asked. Soumya guided him to Teena's room while Deepak remained in the living area.

Roy was reminded of Teena's theory as he stood in the space which housed her being. He was now in that space which knew her intimately. It was even aware of the secret that she kept from him, about which he learned some time before from Deepak. Roy realised that the room was closer to Teena than he was and a twinge of envy flashed through his mind. Brushing it aside, he slowly examined the room, looking at every nook and cranny without giving his eyes a chance to miss anything. They suddenly rested on her table where she had neatly arranged some documents. "Teena asked me not to touch her books and files before she left," Soumya commented. Roy took Teena's travel bag that sat on the floor and put her notepad, papers and files inside. He turned and looked passively at a perplexed Saumya before heading out with Deepak.

It was almost nine at night when Roy reached his home. As soon as he opened the door, he kept Teena's bag down and sat down on the sofa closing his eyes. It had been quite some time since he went on such long drives. The uneven roads contributed more to his tiredness and his back ached due to prolonged sitting. Despite his body's craving for some rest, he took out a bulky file from the bag and opened it. *Realities of Yesterday* by Teena Roy.

The title of the novel that Teena was writing, her little suspense that she told him about during the weekend. He proceeded to the prologue and started reading his wife's first novel disregarding his drowsy eyes.

Roy did not know how many hours passed when he suddenly heard footsteps coming from the bedroom. "How is it?" Teena asked. "Amazing," replied Roy. "It is good that you chose to write it as fiction rather than a biography. This is going to be a huge success. I'm confident." Teena blushed, ecstatic. "Write the rest of it soon," he encouraged her further. "I need Rajagopal to tell me the rest of the story. That's why I went to find him," she said. "Why did you switch off your phone?" he asked, his tone suddenly turning gloomy. "Don't you know I'll be tensed if I can't reach you?" "I lost my phone. Somebody pushed me from behind, Roy. It fell somewhere in the forest."

The file fell down from the hands of the reader who had fallen into a deep sleep. Roy jolted awake when he felt it slip out of his hands. *I didn't ask her where she was*, he thought. He pondered if he should start trusting his dreams like Teena did rather than considering them as a handicap in his life.

Since he knew that he could not keep himself conscious any longer, Roy decided to call it a day and walked to his bedroom with Teena's manuscript in his hand. He kept the file safely on the table, took his bottle of medicines and proceeded to open its cap when he suddenly halted as though he had finally come to a conclusion. Throwing the bottle into the dustbin, he moved towards the window and stared outside where some days back he saw the girl who gave him information about the 'missing ones'. "Anybody who wants to talk to me can come now," he said. "I don't care whether you are a dream, a hallucination or a ghost. I just need to know where my Teena is."

CHAPTER 23

Roy searched inside the refrigerator for the last two pieces of bread that he had kept aside the other day. He overslept last night due to fatigue and woke up well past breakfast time. The sound of footsteps outside his home made Roy stop and listen. He closed the door of the refrigerator, looked outside through his window and spotted three policemen wandering around the premises. Before he had time to think, the doorbell rang.

CI Ajith and SI Asif walked in through the front door as Roy stood aside to let them pass. Ajith scanned the house like a prospective buyer and lightly touched a money plant kept on the window sill. "This is an old construction, isn't it? You have maintained it well," he observed. Roy smirked. "Glad that you decided to investigate my case three days after my wife disappeared." He headed to the table where he kept the documents that he had brought from Teena's apartment while the confused officers followed him. "See," he said pointing towards the table. "There is the collection of documents, photographs and files which mark important events in the life of author Rajagopal. And that is Teena's unfinished manuscript." Ajith and Asif looked at each other. "This is how Teena and Rajagopal are acquainted. She is writing his life story. He had been narrating it to her until he vanished. They had planned to publish it next month through Teena's friend Deepak's publishing house." Roy took a moment to inspect the officers' expressions and explained further "Why is the story of Rajagopal written in confidentiality? And, why did Rajagopal, who knows many world-famous publishers, choose to publish the book in a relatively new firm?" Seeing that there was still no response from the other side, he continued more emphatically, "You must take my words seriously. Rajagopal wants to reveal some of his secrets through Teena's novel. That's why they both went missing just before she wrote the last and the most crucial part. Someone doesn't want the world to know what Rajagopal wishes to share." "Who?"

asked Asif who had been keenly listening to Roy. "That's for you officers to find out," Roy retorted, relieved that they finally started to believe him. "You should understand that two lives are in danger. Please start doing something to find them at least from now. There is no use stalking me and searching my house," he added confidently.

Ajith could not take it any longer. He was fed up with listening to Roy and his imaginary tales. Least bothered about keeping his emotions from his voice, he said, "Stop living inside your dream world and come to your senses! Rajagopal was found yesterday evening. Switch on the television and see for yourself!" Roy gazed at him in disbelief. "It is not like what you think, Roy," said Asif in a much softer tone. "Rajagopal seemed to have lost his way when he went to visit a friend. One of his relatives found him in a primary health centre in a village in Tamil Nadu and informed his son. He is currently admitted to the Alpha Care Hospital, Ernakulam." Roy stood there transfixed, breathing fast, with his eyes glued to the floor. He had become hopeful the previous night when he was able to gather some evidence about Rajagopal's connection with Teena but now he knew that since Rajagopal was already found, the police would not give much importance to Teena anymore.

Ajith shook his head and walked towards the door signalling Asif to follow him. As he reached the door, he turned back and said, "We have taken up Teena's case seriously enough. She has been missing for three days and we have not received any information about her. So, I believe that she has gone on her own accord. Or," he added more as a warning than a promise, "like you said, if there is someone behind all these, I'll make sure that we bring him before the law."

The police vehicle gathered speed as it passed the gates of Roy's home. He could not understand what was going on. If Rajagopal was at the hospital now, where did Teena go? Roy switched on the television and pressed some buttons on the remote control. 'Breaking News: Renowned author Rajagopal in critical condition' flashed on the screen. A group of reporters crowded around Rajagopal's son Sreenivas Rajagopal who was also a celebrated MLA, stretching out their different coloured microphones as near to him as possible so that they would not miss even a single word he uttered.

"Papa often told us that he wanted to visit some of his friends but we didn't let him go because the doctors have advised him against travelling. He has been suffering from certain health issues lately due to his age," Sreenivas explained, trying to remain calm in spite of being maddened by the many numbers of mikes and cameras before him. "Is it true that he was planning to resume his writing?" asked a reporter who had managed to push through the gathering to the front. "How is his health right now? Is there any hope for recovery?" another voice shouted from the middle, extending a red-coloured mike as far as her bangled hand could reach. "What do you expect?" the son snapped and walked away angrily, turning a deaf ear to the countless incomprehensible questions coming from the crowd for whom it was an integral part of their lives to get some information from the sensations of the day in order to sustain themselves in the job that provided them with their daily bread.

Roy heard the sound of his mobile phone ringing and he looked at the screen hoping against hope to see the name of his wife on it. Despite being downhearted when he saw that the caller was Deepak, he took it, swiped the green icon up and turned on the speaker.

"Hello," Roy said, his voice barely audible.

"Soumya and I are at the hospital. We are trying our best to see Rajagopal."

"What's the point in visiting someone who is on his deathbed?"

"We'll speak to his family and find out where he had gone. We are doing all we can."

Roy had no energy left in him to speak. Cutting the call, he sat on the sofa staring at the television screen, mindlessly watching the reporters give their opinions on the matter. He did not even notice Nabeesumma coming in with two steel vessels containing his lunch. She kept them on the teapoy and stood by the door as she did not have the heart to ask him anything.

"… Rajagopal preferred to have a private life after his novel *Selvi* was published. It has been nearly twenty years since we saw him in a public function…" the television continued.

CHAPTER 24

Ajith asked Asif to pull over as he wanted to have a smoke. While he had almost concluded that there was no connection between Rajagopal's and Teena's cases, Teena's manuscript had once again jumbled up the pieces of the puzzle. He got out of the car, stretched his arms and then took out a packet of cigarettes from his shirt pocket. As he slowly took a drag of his cigarette, Asif came and stood beside him.

"What do you think?" Ajith asked.

"Teena's manuscript and those documents confirm that she was writing the story of author Rajagopal," Asif replied.

"And."

"I was just wondering... let's picture things

from Roy's point of view."

"Go on," Ajith encouraged.

"What if somebody doesn't want some truths to be revealed? What if author Rajagopal was indeed abducted and left in this condition?"

"If that is so, the same people might have kidnapped Teena as well so that her book will not see the light of the day. Isn't it?" Ajith asked.

"Yes," Asif said.

"Then why didn't they kill them both?" Ajith asked.

"Perhaps all they want is to stop the book from getting published."

"So, you think the book might be about some crime that they committed along with Rajagopal. Rajagopal now wants to confess it through the book but the others fear that their part will also be exposed if the book comes out. Right?"

"Yes, sir," Asif said.

"You do read a lot of thriller novels, don't you?"

Ajith asked, smiling.

"I watch movies," Asif admitted sheepishly.

"I want the investigation report of Rajagopal's case as soon as possible," Ajith said, suddenly turning serious.

"I'll get it sir," Asif replied.

"Good, let's go then," Ajith said as he put out his cigarette and stretched his upper body again.

As the vehicle started to move, the CI looked out of the window and immersed himself in deep thought. Even though he dismissed Asif's findings and held crime fiction works responsible for his thoughts, Ajith could not completely deny that there was a possibility that what Asif came up with might be the actual story. However, he was sure that Roy had some involvement in the case. Ajith was not a person who believed in powers that were said to be beyond the comprehension of human beings. He could not accept the existence of inexplicable capabilities that some people claimed that they had. Knowingly or unknowingly, Roy was in some way responsible for Teena's disappearance. As a police officer, it was

his duty to find out what actually happened to
Teena.

CHAPTER 25

Roy drove fast as he was eager to inform the police everything he had learned the previous night, or rather, early that morning. Even slight hindrances on the road incensed him and he honked his horn now and then like an enraged animal warning its opponents to back off. He was sure that this was going to be a turning point in Teena's missing case and desperately hoped that the police would believe him this time.

Several knocks on the door woke Roy up last night when tiredness and despair had pushed him into somnolence quite early. His heart thumped fast as the noise had startled him awake and he rubbed his eyes to ward off the last traces of sleep from them. "Coming," he said as he got up from the bed and hurried towards the door. As usual, he half expected Teena's warm hug as he opened the door but was disappointed to see that it was not her but a stranger who stood before him. However, his heartbeat escalated once more when he recognised the person, the middle-aged man who was standing behind Rajagopal's son and whispering into his ear while he was addressing the media.

"You are journalist Teena's husband, aren't you?" he asked.

"Yes," replied Roy suspiciously.

"I'm Rajagopal's relative, Narayanan. I stay at the hospital with him during nights."

Roy nodded wondering what this man was doing at his house at this hour if he was supposed to be at the hospital with Rajagopal.

"Rajagopal wishes to talk to you. He told me that the things he wants you to know can't wait," he said, sounding urgent.

"But the media said that Rajagopal was in a bad state," Roy began doubtfully but Narayanan cut him short.

"Please come fast. There is not much time. The

hospital will be surrounded by people as soon as the dawn breaks."

While sitting in the rear seat of the taxi in which Narayanan had come, Roy was still unsure if he should have gotten inside a vehicle with someone he was not acquainted with. As the car passed speedily through the dark and quiet road, he posed his question again.

"Can Rajagopal talk? I heard that he is in a coma and is put on a ventilator."

"That's all a lie. There is nothing wrong with him except that he is fatigued. But we can't say that to the media. If the word is out that Rajagopal can talk, he will be killed."

"Why?" asked Roy, shaken.

"If he talks, he will reveal everything. You know, even those incidents that happened during the prime of his life." He laughed uncomfortably. "He is like that these days."

The roads were almost deserted as it was already long past midnight. Roy felt that they reached the hospital pretty fast and he doubted if he had dozed off in between. The taxi driver dropped them in front of the portico and Narayanan paid him off. "We can't go through the main entrance. The security guard is there," he said, turning towards Roy. "Come with me."

Roy followed him through the dimly lit grounds of Alpha Care Hospital. When they walked further, a bright light shone on Roy's face and he looked up to see a luminous sign board above an ATM booth. "This way," said Narayanan pointing towards a white door by the side of the booth on which was written 'STAFF ONLY' in bold red. He opened the door for Roy and motioned him to proceed through the stairway that lay ahead.

The flickering blue light inside and the eerie silence made Roy's blood run cold. When he reached the top of the stairs, he looked back to find that Narayanan was no longer with him. He tentatively moved forward through the straight corridor lighted up by a strange pink-coloured electric bulb and reached a point where the path bifurcated. As he stood watching each one alternately wondering which would lead him to Rajagopal, a nurse came out of nowhere, smiled at him and signalled to him to continue through the one on his left. Before going much forward he saw a room with its door ajar which he pushed open and found Rajagopal in bed. "I was waiting for you," he said, his eyes on the ceiling. The beeping sound of the heart monitor and the bright yellow and pink bulbs on either side of the room which were switched on together made Roy sick. However, ignoring his discomfort, he leaned towards the author to listen to him.

"Tell Teena to complete the book fast," said Rajagopal.

"Do you know where she is?" Roy asked, unaware that his voice was too loud and inappropriate for an ICU room.

"She... She is in the forest."

"Where?" Roy encouraged, his hopes high.

"We killed her... buried her," Rajagopal said faintly.

"What!" Roy exclaimed as his heart skipped a beat.

"Tell Teena to write everything... She shouldn't leave out anything," Rajagopal continued.

Roy heaved a sigh of relief. "Whom did you kill?" he asked.

All of a sudden, Roy heard footsteps outside and two nurses along with a security guard appeared at the door. They looked shocked as though he was a thief whom they caught in the middle of his work. Without a word, the guard held him by the collar of his shirt, dragged him and threw him out of the room. Hitting his head hard against the wall, Roy felt a sharp pain shooting through his face before he lost consciousness.

CHAPTER 26

The four men inside the police vehicle had different things running inside their heads. Roy was thinking only about finding Teena as soon as possible, Asif was astounded that Ajith decided to believe Roy, Ajith wanted to somehow get this case out of his head and Suresh who joined them from Ernakulam upon the request of his friend was more or less indifferent to the situation. The jeep came to a halt in the same place that Roy alighted last night when Narayanan brought him to visit Rajagopal. Roy assumed that Rajagopal would be able to open up more now, without the interference of the hospital staff, since he had come with three important officials of the police department.

"You wait outside," Ajith told Roy as he, Asif

and Suresh rushed in through the main entrance, heading towards the reception. Roy watched them until they vanished around the corner. Even though he supposed that the police would unearth the secrets hidden in the depths of the author's mind, he feared that Rajagopal would refuse to cooperate with them. He doubted whether Rajagopal wanted only Teena and himself to know the truths before his heart reached the public in the form of printed words. As Roy stood there trusting that Rajagopal's confession would lead them to Teena, the person who knocked at his door last night walked past him with a flask in his hand. Thinking that the man did not notice him, Roy ran after him and stopped him.

"Good morning, Narayanan. I told the police everything Rajagopal told me yesterday," Roy said, offering him a handshake. He looked at Roy questioningly. "What are you talking about? Are you crazy? Rajagopal is in a coma! And my name is not Narayanan. I am Xavier," he shouted. "God! Why am I wasting my time talking to you!" he murmured to himself before storming off. Roy was appalled. The person in front of him was not the one who spoke to him yesterday; his voice and mannerisms differed greatly from the Narayanan whom he knew.

Roy took his steps slowly, with his legs trembling uncontrollably, to the ATM booth beside the main entrance. His heart started to palpitate when he saw that in the place of the door with the red letters, there was only a blank wall next to the booth, and it seemed to him as if it stood as an obstacle to solving the mystery of Teena's disappearance. Every sign of life vanished from Roy's face. He cursed himself for disregarding his mental disorder. In his desperation, he took out his phone and touched on Teena's name from his contacts once again. However, to his utmost surprise and joy, he heard her caller tune from the other end instead of the recorded voice that announced that the phone was switched off. Even though she did not pick up the call, it was a ray of hope for him who felt just a moment before that he was back to square one. Like a traveller who found an oasis when he thought that he was lost in a parched desert, he almost jumped with ecstasy and forgot the fact that he would have to face the consequences of causing trouble to the police.

Ajith gritted his teeth in anger as he walked

out of the ICU. He knew that he had no one but himself to blame for the embarrassment that he just faced. His wrath automatically quickened his pace and he did not bother whether the other two were following him or not. Suresh tried to keep up with his friend, attempting to soothe him with consoling words. Asif, on the other hand, had already begun to worry about how the CI would take out his anger on Roy.

As soon as Roy saw the trio coming out of the hospital building, he ran to them stretching out his mobile phone. "Teena's phone rang," he shouted in excitement. Ajith glared at him and commanded, "Get inside the jeep." "I'll drive," he then said to Asif who had almost reached the driver's seat. The rage in Ajith's eyes reminded Roy how he had misled the officers and wasted their time. Without making the situation any worse, he got into the back seat with Asif. Suresh eyed his friend from time to time while Ajith sped through the traffic, swearing at almost every driver on the road.

Roy turned on the speaker when he called Teena this time since he wanted the police to understand that her phone did ring when he tried calling her number while they were at the hospital. But fortune did not appear to favour him that day; the same, dispiriting voice that had been breaking the poor husband's heart for days spoke again to inform the listeners that Teena's phone was switched off.

"I-I really heard it ring," he stammered.

"Shut up!" Ajith snapped, striving hard to control his voice. "Get yourself admitted to a mental asylum if you are sick! Why do you roam around and cause trouble?" He paused, sighed and continued, "I should have arrested you for attempting to spread gossip about a popular author. God! Why did I trust this madman in the first place!"

Taking an abrupt right turn, Ajith drove the vehicle into a narrow lane, with brick walls on both sides, away from the main road. Suresh and Asif looked around, perplexed at what he was doing but neither dared to frame their concern into a question. Roy who was still calling Teena's number was unaware of what was happening outside. Everybody was thrown forward when Ajith suddenly slammed on the brakes.

The small path had led them to a deserted, wide, overgrown area which looked like a wasteland. Ajith pulled over to the left side, got out and lighted a cigarette. Asif and Suresh also got down from the vehicle and stood near Ajith, carefully forming sentences in their minds to calm him down before actually verbalising them. Roy decided to break the silence and spoke. "You're right, I'm mad. But where is my wife? It has been many days since she went missing. Why can't the police find her yet?" "I wonder how she tolerated you for ten years," Ajith retorted. "I am damn sure that she left you because she couldn't stand you any longer." He took another puff, threw the cigarette on the ground, put it out using his boot and got back inside the jeep. Roy was not ready to let it go. "I came to your house in the middle of the night and made everything clear to you the first time you made this statement," he said. Ajith looked at Asif and Suresh as though he was completely clueless about what Roy was talking about. "You can fake ignorance. I can't and don't want to prove anything. But one thing I want to tell you is that if you approach the case with a prejudiced mind, you'll never find my Teena." Ajith shook his head, closed his eyes and took several deep breaths. Asif slowly moved towards Roy, looked at him kindly and said, "Roy, the apartment that he lives in is not somewhere you can freely enter. You have to get special permission from the security officer even to set foot inside the gates."

CHAPTER 27

Asif always felt calm when he saw the small endless hills of tea plantations in Munnar, especially after spending a day in a busy city. He was sure that the lovely roads with their twists and turns would not ever fail to entrance him. Born and brought up in such a heaven, it was his biggest desire to live and even have his final rest there. The hectic city life never attracted him. According to him, no other place could be called his home. He lowered the window of the jeep to let the pure, cool air in. Forgetting the pressures of the day for a while, he smiled to himself and even considered humming a favourite tune.

All of a sudden, it pricked his conscience to feel good since the man sitting beside him was full of despondence. After dropping Suresh at his station and Ajith at his apartment, Asif had invited Roy to sit in the front passenger seat. They were on their way to the place where Roy's car was parked. With a pang of guilt, he glanced at Roy and was alarmed to see that the man had fixed his eyes on the road ahead with no expression in them. He looked as good as dead.

"Roy?" he called.

"Mm?" Roy asked, startled.

"Please don't worry. CI Ajith is a good man and a skilful officer," Asif explained. "He has solved a lot of cases which were even more complicated. It is just that he has some anger issues."

"I know that my condition will cause trouble to everyone but what other choice do I have? Only Teena can tell me what is real and what is not. I have nobody else in this world." Roy wiped his eyes on the sleeves of his shirt. "Do you remember the first time Ajith Ishwar told me that my wife left me? His words devastated me. Have you thought about what would have happened if I started having dreams about my wife leaving me; if my mind convinced me that what he told me was true? Who else would have been there to save her?"

Asif looked at him wordlessly and he continued.

"Fortunately I saw our friend Dr. Ashwathy that day. She's the only person who knows everything about us, how much Teena and I love each other. She knows that Teena would never even think of abandoning me. If not for the confidence that she gave me, I wouldn't have set out on this investigation."

Asif furrowed his brows in confusion and was about to say something but he immediately decided against it. He stopped the jeep on the side of the road behind Roy's car. Roy alighted, turned back to face Asif and said, "This might be another unsolved mystery for you, one you would forget when the trail gets cold. But I will do everything I can to find my Teena. I won't give up. I can't live without her."

When he was sure that Roy was out of earshot, Asif took a blue diary from the dashboard of the jeep, opened it and started searching inside scrupulously. He hurriedly turned the pages, running his eyes through each, and finally stopped at the one where several phone numbers were written. He had not saved Dr Ashwathy's number in his mobile phone since he did not think that he would need it again. After dialling the digits, he held the phone to his ear. He did not have to wait long for her to pick up the call.

"Hello."

"Hello, Dr Ashwathy. I'm sub-inspector Asif. I called you some days before regarding Teena's case."

"Yes, I remember. Is there any news about her?"

"No, we're trying our best. I wanted to ask you something."

"Please do," she said.

"I saw on your Facebook page that you work in Delhi. Did you come to Munnar recently?"

"No, I haven't gone anywhere this month. Why?" she asked.

"Nothing. Just wanted to know. Thank you," he replied.

It was long past dusk and Asif was too tired to go back to work. He drove reluctantly, pondering about the strange condition of the person who had been travelling with him from the morning. It was only when he was with Roy for almost a day did he realise how terrible Roy's illness was. Roy's life seemed like fiction to him. He wondered how his department was going to unravel this case if they did not know whether or not to believe the statements of the complainant.

Parking the vehicle on the vast ground outside the police station, Asif ascended the steps thinking about the tasks that needed his immediate attention. As he entered the door, the assistant sub inspector stood up, saluted him in haste and said, "An officer from the cyber cell called almost two hours ago; he asked you to call him as soon as you were back." Asif nodded and proceeded to his room. He took the receiver of his office land phone, dialled the number and waited.

"Hello, this is SI Asif," he initiated straightaway as he was eager to know what the department wanted to notify him. His instincts told him that the call had something to do with Teena. "Sir, the mobile number that you gave us, journalist Teena's, was switched on for some time today noon but no calls were made," a male voice informed. "We traced the location and it showed a forest area near the Kerala-Tamil Nadu border, a place called Chinnathodu."

CHAPTER 28

Thangavel knew that the police thought he had intended to keep the mobile phone. Though he was poor and his whole family, which consisted of his wife, two children and his elderly parents, lived on his sole income, he would never desire a single thing that belonged to another. Never in his life did he compare himself to someone else. He was always contented with whatever he had and was grateful for everything to the supreme power in which he believed.

The forest guard's house was in the middle of the scenic woods. When he got the job at the age of twenty-one, he was overjoyed since he knew that he could live, perhaps forever, in the jungle which was not alien to him. He grew up on the lap of the forest and was fonder of the flora and fauna than of the members of his own species. The land was a second mother to him and he considered it his great fortune to get a chance to take care of it.

It was not the first time that someone from his family had found such things in the woods. Once, his mother got a gold pendant and Thangavel dutifully returned it to the police the next time he went to the city. He knew the agony of losing cherished belongings and he never intended to inflict such a pain on anyone. It hurt him to think that the police still suspected he would keep something he got from the forest. He could not bear to be called a thief when he was making a decent living from his hard-earned job.

That night, almost around eight, Thangavel saw from his window, two policemen approaching his house. He knew both of them. It was no secret to anyone who was acquainted with them that they hated Thangavel and he reciprocated their feelings for him. He muttered a curse under his breath not just because their arrival meant trouble but also because he had just washed his hands and hungrily sat in front of his supper. The delectable combination of tapioca and fish curry prepared according to his liking by his wife tempted him to ignore everything else and dig into the food on his plate. But he was sure he could not. He had no other choice. Wiping his wet hands on his *lungi*, he got up from his chair, put on a shirt and opened the door with a fake smile on his face.

"Hey, Thangavel!"

"Good evening, sir. It has been a long time," Thangavel replied, making sure that he sounded friendly.

"We got a call from the Kerala police about a missing case," the junior inspector said, ignoring his pleasant remark. "It seems that a woman got lost somewhere inside this forest." He handed his mobile phone to Thangavel and asked, "Have you seen her anywhere?"

Thangavel looked closely at Teena's picture on the officer's mobile phone and remembered the photo that he saw on the mobile phone that his wife got from the jungle the other day. He asked the policemen to wait, ran inside and came back with it. The senior officer took the phone from him eyeing him distrustfully. "My wife found it. I was planning to give it to the police station tomorrow when I come to the city. It has that woman's picture in it," Thangavel explained. The officers looked at each other and exchanged a sceptical smile. Thangavel clenched his fists to suppress his annoyance and explained further. "It was switched off when we got it. I turned it on this morning but switched it off again when it started ringing." The officer switched on the phone and saw the picture of Teena leaning against Roy's shoulder on its lock screen. "All right, Thangavel. We'll inform the Kerala police that the forest guard had the woman's phone with him." He smirked and then turned and walked away followed by the junior inspector who scanned Thangavel from head to toe before leaving.

Such hostile attitudes from the people around him were not new to Thangavel. As a person who had to face a lot in his life, this was nothing. He knew that they were not going to report anything against him to the Kerala police and that trying to frighten him was only one of their ways of amusement. He used to fall for such tricks before but now he did not pay any heed to them. It did not bother him even if they planned to present him as a villain. Smiling to himself, he hurried back to his supper which his wife had covered with another plate to protect the food from insects that were hovering around the light bulb. "How many times have I told you to keep the door closed? You don't know how difficult it is to get rid of those things once they get inside," his wife complained as she hastened to close the front door before she had to deal with more of the flying creatures who came to visit their bright lover hanging from the ceiling of the human's home.

CHAPTER 29

Nabeesumma quickly packed some *cherupayar kanji*, rice gruel with green grams, in a steel container and rushed towards Roy's house when she heard the sound of his car. He had informed her in the morning that he might not be back before night and that he would have happy news for her very soon. However, when she saw him, it did not look like he had anything good to share. She kept the food on the table and stood in front of the dejected figure who sat on the sofa with his face buried in his hands. "I can't tell you anything now, *umma*," he said. A drop of tear wetted the mother's cheek as she left the son alone. When Roy married Teena, she thought that since God had tested the boy enough, He was going to shower him with blessings from then on. Nabeesumma wondered why the All-Merciful tormented such a humble soul as Roy. She prayed with all her heart for Teena's safety and for peace to be returned to her son's family.

Roy did not look up until he was sure that Nabeesumma was not there. He did not want the old woman to see the state he was in. Even though the incidents of the day rendered him downhearted and miserable, he pledged to himself that he was not going to give up until he found Teena. With that determination, he stood up and headed to their bedroom where he had kept her manuscript and the documents he had collected from her apartment in Ernakulam. Scanning through a file, he looked again at the old picture of author Rajagopal in a forest in which he seemed to be laughing his head off with his friends sitting beside a campfire. Immediately, as if he remembered something important, Roy took his phone and called Deepak's number.

"Hello, Roy!"

"Deepak, I need you to listen to me carefully and believe what I say. Do not ask me anything before I complete."

"All right," Deepak replied dubiously.

"Teena is inside a forest. She told me that she lost her phone in a forest. She's in danger. I talked to Rajagopal yesterday and he told me the same as well. Teena has also written in her manuscript that Rajagopal had the habit of visiting a forest near his college with his friends."

"Roy, actually I am at Vazhikkadavu. In my blind search, I somehow reached this place," Deepak continued, "And you're right. There is a forest ahead."

"Then I'll come there." Roy started searching for a pen after putting the call on speaker. "Tell me the exact place you're in."

As he took out a pen from Teena's notepad which was close at hand, Roy saw that on the page where the pen rested, she had noted down some names and had drawn lines connecting them.

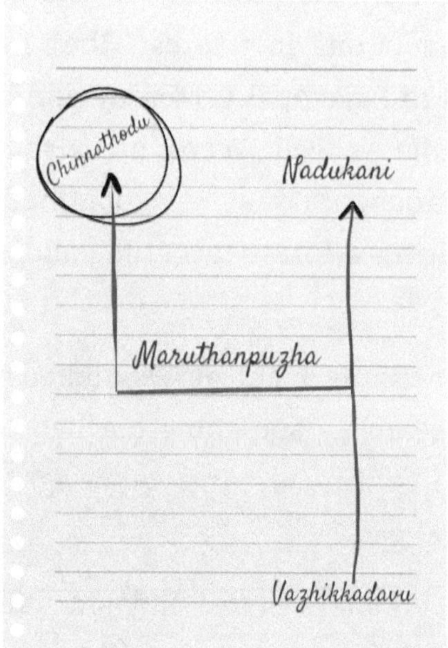

Vazhikkadavu, Nadukani, Maruthanpuzha, Chinnathodu. Those names did ring a bell with Roy. He thought hard about how they sounded so familiar. "Roy? Are you there? Shall I send you my location?" Deepak shouted from the other end but his words appeared only as indecipherable sounds to Roy, which served as nothing but an irksome noise which prevented him from concentrating. He pressed the red coloured icon on the mobile phone screen as if he were under a spell and kept staring at the names on the page. Suddenly everything started coming back to him; the knock on the window, the teenage girl...

"Shall I tell you where the missing ones are? On the way from Vazhikkadavu to Nadukani, towards the left, there is Maruthanpuzha. From Maruthanpuzha, on the way to Chinnathodu, after the check post, there is a big board with a picture of an elephant on it. Go right, and there is a route to the forest where you will find an old house. The missing ones are there."

Roy started breathing faster and his heart pounded with excitement. This was what he had been trying to remember from the day Teena went missing. Without wasting another moment, he took the notepad and hastened towards the front door, grabbing both his house and his car keys from the teapoy on the way. Getting into the car, he sent a short WhatsApp message to Naseema to inform Nabeesumma that he was going in search of Teena and that this time he would really come back with her.

CHAPTER 30

Asif waited beside Ajith as he was doing his daily morning cardio exercise in the gym on the top floor of his apartment complex. The posh residence had every facility one could dream of – from eye-catching abodes to an upscale restaurant on the last floor. Finely polished equipment, some of which Asif was not even vaguely familiar with, gleamed in the yellow LED panel lights artfully arranged on the ceiling. Even though he had been in that room before, he did not fail to marvel at it each time he stepped inside.

As the treadmill slowly came to a halt, Ajith signalled Asif to pass him the towel and he wiped off his sweat before seating himself beside the sub-inspector. Realising that Ajith was ready to listen again, Asif continued from where he left off, "We will have to ask the Tamil Nadu police to search around the area where Teena's mobile phone was found. The whole forest needs to be thoroughly searched, it seems. I have already shared Teena's photograph and details with every police station between Munnar and Chinnathodu. I will be leaving for Chinnathodu shortly." Ajith leaned his head on the wall and remained silent for a while before he responded. "So this leads us to Roy's story, doesn't it?" Asif nodded. Working with the CI for more than three years, he could easily read his senior officer like an open book and the man's reluctance to be defeated by Roy did not go unnoticed by him. "What did our petitioner say?" Ajith asked as he straightened himself and looked at Asif. "Actually I haven't spoken to him about it yet," Asif said tentatively. "Since we didn't get a clear picture, I thought…" "What if your 'clear picture' is not good?" Ajith cut in. "Call him and tell him to come to the station," he ordered. "I was rather rude to him last time. I need you to pacify him." "Sure sir," Asif replied. "And start for Chinnathodu as soon as possible after that," added Ajith.

It took a little while before Roy answered

Asif's phone and the latter suspected that the receiver would not entertain any more calls from the police. "Hello," the dull hurried voice said as though it was not interested to waste time in small talk.

"Hello, Roy! CI Ajith wants to talk to you about something very important. Can you come to the station today morning?"

"I can't. I'm sorry," came the curt reply. "I am not there in Munnar."

"Where are you then?"

"I am going to Chinnathodu."

"Did you say Chinnathodu?" asked Asif, astonished.

"Teena is there, inside a forest," Roy replied.

"How do you know that?"

Nothing more was heard from the other end and the shocked officer held his mobile phone to his ear a minute more before he turned to face Ajith who was looking at him perplexed. "What happened?" he asked. "He is on his way to Chinnathodu," Asif responded mechanically. Ajith tried to hide a triumphant smile. "I knew it!" he said. "I knew that he was the one behind this drama. That scoundrel was putting on an act in front of us all these days. He might have understood that we are about to crack the case and then he comes with a new twist." Ajith stood up and placed the towel on his shoulder. "You came by your car, didn't you?" he asked. "Yes," said Asif. "I'm coming with you to Chinnathodu. We need to reach there immediately," Ajith declared. "Let me go and have a quick shower."

It was for the first time that Asif saw his superior compete with someone. According to him, Ajith was the epitome of perfection when it came to professional life. There was neither a single mystery that disturbed the officer's mind nor a single case that earned him a disgrace. However, now, the confidence in the CI's eyes had given way to envy and fear of failure. Asif wanted the old version of Ajith Ishwar back and he prayed that this day would somehow mark the end of Teena's case.

"We might find Teena dead or alive today," Ajith said as he walked towards the exit of the gym. Asif stared at him wondering if Ajith heard his thoughts. "Whatever happens," he continued, "we must catch Roy." He strode towards the door, held it open and added, "I will force him to show his true colours."

CHAPTER 31

If not for the delay at the checkpost, Roy would have reached Chinnathodu earlier. The Tamil Nadu police held him there for an unnecessarily long period of time which made him suspect that the police of his own state had a hand in it. He thought to himself that he should never have let the police know where he was. The thickets on both sides of the road moved in the breeze as if they were welcoming him to their home. Turning on the headlights, Roy slowed down the vehicle and concentrated on the road so that he would not lose his way inside the wilderness. The girl's words kept echoing in his head. Suddenly, he applied the brakes as he gazed through the windshield at the board with the picture of an elephant on it.

Roy pulled over towards the side of the road, got out and headed into the forest. It took some time before his eyes adjusted themselves to the darkness. He took his steps carefully through the dried leaves while he also made sure that he missed nothing on the path. As he walked further, he felt a shaft of sunlight fall on him and he lifted his head to see its source.

The ancient, dilapidated construction, the one that the girl mentioned, stood in front of him as if it was looking straight at him, showing off itself as the very embodiment of everything evil. A single glance at that horrendous structure would inevitably make even the bravest person shudder. Nobody would want to be anywhere in its vicinity. However, Roy knew that Teena would have felt excited when she discovered it in the middle of the jungle. She would not have been afraid. The determination of the woman and her dedication towards her novel would have tricked her brain into shutting out the basic instinct of fear which was necessary to protect oneself from impending danger.

Roy headed towards the building unaware that Ajith and Asif, along with some constables from Tamil Nadu, were behind him, maintaining a safe distance so that he would not sense that he was being followed. Ajith was sure that Roy would provide ample evidence against himself that day, whereby the officer could prove he had always been right on his judgement. Keeping his gaze fixed on Roy, Ajith led the team into the heart of the woods and went after him inside the ramshackle house. The CI became pretty sure this was the place where Roy had hidden his wife.

Without a warning, the police pushed Roy aside and walked past him, leaving him nonplussed. A quick thought made him comprehend why he was blocked at the checkpost. Ajith, who had stayed behind to let the rest of the team pass, glared at Roy as though he was watching a dangerous criminal. "Where is Teena?" he asked. Roy smirked at him pitying the silliness of such an experienced police officer and entered the building without giving him another glance. Ajith rushed after Roy and grabbed him by the collar of his shirt. "Don't act smart. I know what you are hiding behind that handsome face of yours. Don't you ever dream that you can fool me! I will tear up that mask and let the whole world know who you are. Now stay back!"

Roy lost his balance and fell down as Ajith angrily pushed him before walking away. Even though he was stunned for a moment due to the CI's behaviour, he immediately got up and joined the policemen who were thoroughly searching all over the place. He walked behind them since he did not want to disturb their search but was at the same time eager to catch a glimpse of each room as he was impatient to know if his investigation bore fruit. "Sir," a constable's voice came from the left side. The search party ran towards the voice closely followed by the anxious husband. "Call the ambulance," Roy heard Ajith's voice command.

As he pushed through the uniformed men, Roy found his beloved among the debris on the floor inside a room-like enclosure which had no roof. For a moment he felt a stabbing pain inside his chest as it appeared to him that it was her lifeless body that lay before him. His palpitations made his vision weak and he struggled to get a proper look at his wife. He sat beside her and held his breath trying to find some sign of life in her. Only when he observed the small rise and fall of her chest did he finally heave a sigh of relief. Tears started pouring down his cheeks as he smiled for the first time that week.

CHAPTER 32

"It was on her special request that the doctor agreed to discharge Teena and allowed her to travel back to Munnar," Asif told Ajith as he drove the jeep slowly and carefully through the curved road. Five days had passed since the events inside the forest. The doctor had informed the police that there was no sign of physical abuse or any such attempts. Two constables who went to take Teena's statement at the hospital had reported that Teena was attacked from behind and that she did not have any clue about the people who had locked her up, much to the CI's dismay. He was almost sure that Teena would point the finger at Roy, making his suspicions right but she told the police that she went there for a personal reason that she did not want to reveal. "Even though the doctor wanted her to stay for a week, he said that she was kind of all right now." Ajith nodded to signal that he was listening. "I enquired about Roy's tower location as you said and found that it had not changed at all before Teena went missing. His neighbour also testified that he had never gone anywhere those days." Ajith started and looked at Asif. "I'm sorry sir, your doubts were wrong," Asif said, emphasising his point.

Ajith was not convinced about Roy's innocence, no matter how many alibis Asif provided. He had always felt that Asif had a soft spot for Roy. As a practical man, he could not believe that Roy's intuitions led him to Teena, and that too, when the police were finally on the right track. It would not be easy for Roy to make Ajith strike off his name from the lists of suspects that he had carved inside his mind. Ajith trusted that there was something that he missed, that would have helped him prove Roy's part in what happened to Teena.

"SI Manikandan from Chinnathodu called me. He said that the forest guard didn't know anything. The guard and his family think that the old building is haunted. They never go near it if they can help it," Asif said laughing. "Did you find out anything about that house? To whom it belonged or something?" asked Ajith, disregarding Asif's attempt to lighten the situation. "Someone encroached upon the land and built the house on it long back. It was reclaimed by the forest department in 1992. An interesting fact is that the college Rajagopal studied in is just 15km away from that forest. He and his friends, Xavier, Mathew, Manoj and Ahmad, used to frequent the place. Xavier and Mathew are cousins. Xavier is also now Rajagopal's manager and Rajagopal's son, the MLA, has married Xavier's daughter," Asif explained. "So you do believe what Roy says, don't you?" Ajith posed it more as a statement than a question. "No, sir," Asif replied, taken aback. "I think there is no need for us to investigate this case any further. The missing people have been found. The house and the mysteries surrounding it are not our concern. Let the Tamil Nadu police deal with it." Ajith watched him dubiously and said, "If Roy's story is right and I get my proof to believe it, I want to apologise to him for treating him the way I did. If it is not and he is in some way culpable, I'll not let him escape the hands of the law."

The jeep stopped in front of Roy's home and

Asif got down and opened the gates wide. While Asif was parking the vehicle inside, Ajith tried to recollect the questions that he had prepared to ask Teena. He was worried that the picture that Roy had given her about him would prevent her from opening up. Nevertheless, he was not going to let this case be a black mark against him and he was ready to go to any extent to get to the bottom of it.

Roy opened the door quickly when he heard the doorbell. The melancholic expression on Roy's face had magically vanished and in its place, the visitors saw joy and tranquillity. There was not even a trace of the prior hatred that he exhibited when the police came to visit him last time. It looked as if Teena's presence had chased away the negativity that surrounded the home for the past few days.

"Hello Roy, how's Teena?" Asif asked.

"She's good. A bit tired though, after being locked in the room without food or water for such a long time."

"Actually someone did provide me with food and water," said a voice from the corner of the living room. "When I opened my eyes, there was a packet of eatables and two bottles of water. I might have died if they had decided to dehydrate me for four days straight."

Everybody looked at Teena as she took her steps cautiously towards the living room. Asif and Ajith felt like they were looking at a character from a novel who had suddenly jumped out of the pages and stood in front of them in flesh and blood. Forgetting the surroundings, both of them stared shamelessly at her and it took a few seconds for them to realise how awkward they might have seemed to the couple.

"Hello, Teena," Ajith volunteered to speak so that nobody would notice the embarrassment on his face.

"Hello, please have a seat," she said motioning towards the sofa.

"Let's get straight to the point," Ajith said as he and Asif accepted her invitation and sat down. "Is it true that you went in search of Rajagopal?"

"Yes," Teena replied.

"Then why did you lie to the police that you

were not acquainted with him?" Asif asked.

"I am writing his life story in the form of fiction. I had promised him that I wouldn't speak about it, or even that I know him, to anyone."

"Right," said Ajith. "How are you going to complete your novel when Rajagopal is in a condition like this?"

Teena smiled at the officers indicating that she knew what they were getting at but did not want to answer the question.

"Don't you want the people who harmed you and author Rajagopal to be punished?" Ajith asked bending forward towards Teena as though he was imploring her to say more.

"I do," she replied. "That's why I have decided to complete the book even if Rajagopal is not in a condition to help me."

"Then why are you not cooperating with the police?"

"Well," she said. "I intend to complete the book with whatever Rajagopal has told me," she paused and added, "and with what Roy has seen in his dreams. He has agreed to help me with the rest of my book." She watched Ajith for a moment and said, "Even though many people consider Roy to be a madman, I think that there is something magical in what he sees. I do not have any problem in sharing what I know with the police, but I don't think I can provide any evidence to support my statements."

Ajith sighed.

"I can write whatever I want in my novel. It is fiction. But how can I report those incidents to the police when all I know is what Roy told me from his dreams?"

Ajith was rather impressed with Teena and the way she conveyed her thoughts to him in spite of his disagreement with her faith in her husband's fantasies. The officers got up to leave as they understood that they were not going to get anything more from her. However, as they headed towards the door, Ajith decided that he would contribute something to Teena's novel. The cunning officer also had an ulterior motive; he wanted the culprits, if there were any, to be provoked so that he could make the missing cases a feather in his cap and gain back his former glory once again.

CHAPTER 33

As soon as the officers stepped out, Roy returned to the kitchen as he was in the middle of preparing their lunch with some of Teena's favourite dishes. He was not as eager as Teena to open the files that Ajith had given her, which, he said, would be an asset to her when she resumed writing the rest of her book. The appetizing aroma coming from the kitchen failed to captivate Teena's heart as she had already immersed herself in the papers in front of her on the table. She flicked through the pages until she finally found the pictures of the three girls who were still not found after they were reported to be missing from Chinnathodu, during the period when Rajagopal was doing his graduation in Maruthanpuzha.

Roy came to the living room to check why

the tempting smell of food did not attract his wife who mentioned earlier that day that she missed his cooking. When he found that she was concentrating on the file that the CI had given her, he walked quietly to her side and stood near her without disturbing her. He knew how much the novel meant to her and was mentally prepared to do whatever it took to support her dream.

"Roy, Deepak called me just now," Teena said when she became aware of his presence near her. "He said that Rajagopal's condition is hopeless. He might not survive the night."

Roy stood silently, listening to her.

She stared at the wall as if she was in some deep thought and continued, "I am planning to quit my job. I want to completely concentrate on my writing. Moreover," she said, smiling, "now I need to be here to know the rest of the story."

Roy gazed at her as if he could not trust what he just heard. He wondered if his mind was again playing tricks with him.

"You are not dreaming Roy," Teena said and gave him a peck on his cheek as proof, even though she knew that such actions would not help him to distinguish the real and the unreal. "Like you promised, you should always be with me and support me in my writing. I depend on your visions."

"When have I not done something you asked of me?" he said, smiling.

"Ah, I almost forgot," she said all of a sudden as she grabbed his hand and gently pulled him closer to the table. "Look at these photos. They are girls who have gone missing from Chinnathodu and have not yet been found. Got them from the file that the CI gave me."

Roy's eyes widened as he saw the picture of the first girl. He stopped Teena when she tried to turn the page to show him the other two photographs and continued to observe it intently for some more time. Then, turning to Teena, he pointed at the picture without speaking, as though words were trapped inside his mouth. Teena softly placed her hand on Roy's shoulder to put him at ease and waited for him to collect his wits. "She is the one," he managed to say at last. "She is the one who came here; the one who informed me about the people who went missing," he paused and said, "She looked exactly like this, wore the same clothes, had the same ornaments..."

The eeriness in the frozen, awkward smile of the girl in the photograph appeared to increase fourfold as Teena listened to Roy's words. She wondered if it was really the ghost of the girl whom Roy saw outside their house that night. If it was, why did she show herself to him after all those years of her disappearance? Did she want him to do something for her? Should they expect the visitor again at another darkest hour of the night when they would be in their deep, peaceful sleep cuddling each other?

Whatever it was, Teena did not want to disturb the serenity that she and her husband got back after several days of Roy's valiant fight with everything around him. She decided to temporarily put it out of her mind and held Roy's hand reassuringly. Gradually coming out of his shock, Roy regained his composure, kissed Teena on her forehead and they walked inside hand in hand while Teena started praising her husband's cooking skills, taking a whiff of the food that was getting ready for her in the kitchen.

EPILOGUE

The man appeared half swallowed by darkness as he sat writing in his diary by the flickering light of a single candle. Despite the dimly lit room, Roy could make out the face of the famous author. In fact, after all that had transpired during the past few weeks, he could identify the guilt-ridden face anywhere. As Roy stood observing the scene, the dark figure turned his head towards him, sat pensively for a moment and then stood up and walked out of the room. Roy rushed towards the desk and picked up the diary that still lay open.

21st January 2002

I saw the cover design of my last book today. It looked exactly like I wanted it to be. The new designer indeed did a good job. The silhouette of the girl against the bright light of the full moon reminded me of the day I saw her for the first and last time. Looking at it carefully, I could make out the braids on both sides of her head and the edge of her dhavani which appeared to have moved slightly to her left due to the breeze. I felt a prick of conscience as I observed it and gave my final approval since it served as a cruel reminder of my youthful times and the kind of monster I was.

The pain that I experience cannot be expressed in words. We nipped a life in the bud. We denied her all the earthly pleasures that her future days might have kept in store for her and snatched her life away in the worst manner possible. She now lies buried in front of that house in the dark woods, inside a deep pit, all alone, with worms eating up her beautiful body. We didn't even let her poor mother see her for the last time. The old woman would still be living her life, hopeful that her daughter would return to her one day.

I know that I cannot escape my mental agony even if I escape the law of the state. Perhaps I can be at peace after I complete my period on this planet and take my final breath. When I think about it now, I don't understand how I could commit such heinous acts and feel no remorse back then. I want to open up to someone but they have bought my silence. Had they offered money, I would gladly have rejected it but they bought my silence playing with my emotions. They begged me not to destroy their lives. My son's political career would also be at stake if I say anything now. I have no other choice but to keep mum. The book, I must admit, is, therefore, my pitiful attempt to break free from the images that have been haunting me every night for many years, preventing me from having an uninterrupted sleep.

My publisher asked me to give them the name of the novel so that they could move forward with the publishing process. Unlike my other novels, I did not need a lot of time to come up with an apt title. What else should I call the book that I wrote as a tribute to that teenager but her own lovely name? Little girl, please forgive my repenting soul and accept this as the least that I can do for you. After writing your story, this old man is going to put down the pen that had been his bread and butter for a lifetime.

'Selvi'.

www.ingramcontent.com/pod-product-compliance
Lightning Source LLC
Chambersburg PA
CBHW020916160726
47993CB00005B/1991